MANY ARE CALLED

Pat Arrowsmith

Published in 1998 by Onlywomen Press, Limited
40 St. Lawrence Terrace, London W10 5ST

ISBN 0-906500-59-1

Cover Design © Tyra Till
Typeset by Chris Fayers, Lower Soldon, Holsworthy, Devon.
Printed and bound by Mackays of Chatham plc

Other books by Pat Arrowsmith

Fiction
Jericho (Cresset Press and GMP's Heretic Books)
Somewhere Like This (W.H. Allen, Granada paperback & GMP)
The Prisoner (Journeyman Press)

Memoir
I Should Have Been a Hornby Train (GMP's Heretic Books)

Non-fiction
To Asia in Peace (Sidgwick & Jackson)
The Colour of Six Schools (Society of Friends Race Relations Committee)

Verse
Breakout (Edinburgh University Student Publications Board)
On The Brink (CND)
Thin Ice (London CND)
Nine Lives (Brentham Press)

CPP ✓	CLN ≤ (0)
CBA	CLO
CFU	CMI
CIN	CPE
CKI	CRI
CLE 6 01	CSA
CLH	CSH
CLHH	

Preface

At various times I have spent longer or shorter periods living in communities and groups of one sort or another: boarding schools, colleges, prisons, a peace camp, a US Quaker sponsored do-good project and a residential social casework group. This book was inspired by the last: in the mid-'50s I was, for a short while, a member of a small team of social workers who lived together as a group, attempting to do casework with "problem families" in Liverpool.

So this book both deals with group interrelationships, tensions and leadership and takes a quizzical look at the type of casework attempted by some social workers in the '50s. The book is also an allegory – about situations all of us are apt to find ourselves in, and the dilemmas we all – or most of us – from time to time have to face.

Chapter 1

One Tuesday afternoon I pressed the door-bell. The sunlight, sieved through hot, industrial air, made hot, pale patches on the black brickwork of tall, broken buildings. I pressed firmly but without self-confidence. My fingers played imaginary scales on the cracked woodwork for about five minutes, which felt like fifteen. I pressed again.

Then the door was opened, but not, as I had expected, by someone dressed quietly in grey or fawn but by a high-heeled young person with earings in a neatly pumped out emerald sweater who looked at me with lightly camouflaged uninterest.

"I'm Miss Green," I said.

"Oh you've come for the shoes," she replied unsmiling, "Would you mind waiting a moment." And she went straight back down the passage before I had time to reply.

I waited on the doorstep. Surely I was entitled to enter – but would it be a trifle presumptuous to do so?

A small boy in wellingtons was walking up and down clanging a piece of metal against the railings.

"They're all out," he announced.

Am I relieved or annoyed? I dread meeting them, yet shouldn't they be here to greet me, as curious about me as I am about them?

"How do you know?" I responded, instantly regretting my brusque tone; for was I not from now on to be a great lover of little children?

Another child called out, and he instantly bolted off down the road shouting unintelligibly.

I turned the door-handle. I was entitled to enter – or else to go away and never return.

From the depths of the house I heard steadily approaching shouting and screeching. The young person reappeared dragging a small, smelly, yelling girl in a torn frock.

"Yes Betty, you must go home now," she said. "You can come back tomorrow when the others are here." I stood aside to let them pass, then entered the house. I sat on a wobbly, wooden chair, one of whose legs was shorter than the others, and wondered what to do next. I decided to read and was fumbling in my suitcase when an immense, beef-steak faced young man appeared.

"Oh, I was just waiting," I explained.

"Any tea going?" he asked.

"I'm sorry, I don't know I'm afraid. I've only just come," I answered.

"Well tell them I was round, would you, but I'll be back tomorrow," he said; and off he went.

The sweatered young person then returned without the yelling child.

"I'm so sorry you've been kept waiting like this," she said, looking properly at me for the first time. "You've come for Charly's coat haven't you?"

"But you said something about shoes," I responded.

"Yes, that's right. Coat and shoes. They told me to be sure and not forget about the coat."

"I think there must be some mistake," I said. "I've not come for anything. I'm Miss Green."

She looked blankly at me for a moment then said slowly:

"Oh I see. I'm sorry. When you said who you were I thought you said Mrs Green, who's to come for Charly Dale's things. But I see – you're Hilary Green. We weren't expecting you till five."

So I decided not to arrive till five. There was plenty of time ahead in which to meet and get to know them all. She asked me in for a cup of tea but I declined the offer saying I would wander about for a bit.

"Tea's at half past five," she stated as I left.

Chapter 2

I was back by a quarter past five.

"Do come in Hilary. We're so sorry we were all out when you arrived," said a discreetly twin-set clad girl effusively, smiling broadly as she opened the door. Smiling back, I replied:

"I'm sorry I got here early. I quite thought I'd let you know when I'd be arriving, but perhaps I forgot to."

"I'm Gladys," the girl continued, still beaming. "The others are all down at tea – though we've only just begun." Dropping her voice she added, 'But Monica isn't here of course. She'll be in tomorrow morning. And Godfrey's out seeing to the Pratts who are having a crisis."

I was at once overwhelmed by the immensity of the task ahead: dealing with Pratts in a crisis at tea-time. It might be good and dedicated to forfeit one's tea day after day for the sake of others, but the seeing-to-Pratts-in-a-crisis bit was an alarming prospect.

We were walking down an olive-green passage, and through a half-open door I could hear the sound of bumping and banging.

"Is that some carpentry going on?" I asked. Gladys looked puzzled.

"Carpentry?" she said, then added with a giggle, "Oh you mean the Quiet Room. It's just Betty in there. She likes bumping things and it's good for her so we let her."

Does she mean yelling Betty dragged off earlier by the sweatered young person and told not to return till tomorrow? Why is she back? Doesn't what the sweatered young person says matter?

"I'm sure there'll be something left," Gladys remarked, pausing on the dining-room threshold. Suddenly I felt indignant.

So there should be, seeing they were supposed to have greeted me over two hours ago.

"Oh it doesn't matter at all," I lied. "I'm not really a bit hungry." We went into the dining-room and I didn't feel nervous about meeting them after all.

What they looked like – how old, what sex, how friendly – was so important that curiously I did not at once notice them. Instead I observed that there was marmalade although it was tea-time and that the sweatered young person was not present.

I had expected my first encounter with them to be like an interview: that they would all be seated behind a table and would look searchingly at me with keen interest as I was about to join their group, then ask me a lot of questions. But they did nothing of the sort. Gladys turned away to pour out a cup of tea and I just stood. Nobody took any notice of me. I wondered whether to sit down at the table or wait until invited to do so.

I stood stock-still like this for a moment with my hands in my pockets to keep my fingers still. I was waiting till I had decided what to do next, feeling for a few more seconds the freedom of pre-arrival. Through the fabric of my coat I could feel the firmness of my thighs and for a moment I was aware of myself as a single body: my collar reminded me of my neck; my feet felt firmly socketed in my shoes; my knickers mapped the contours of my groins; my brassière, suspender-belt, told me that I was one piece firmly held together: a solid, single person, about to break down into my constituent parts when, within the next few seconds, they finally focused on me; so that finally I would not be quite myself any more but facets of myself – those facets that more or less willingly I would offer them; those which rightly or wrongly they would attribute to me; and those which may never, or barely, have existed before, which they would induce and develop.

Then I realised that standing like this with my hands stuck in my pockets I must look self-conscious, not self-contained – that I might even be looking stubborn. So I took my hands out of my pockets and approached the table.

"Is it all right if I sit here or is it someone else's place?" I asked a tall, spectacled girl whose eyes might be deep and looking forth or else merely solid and reflecting back.

"Oh no, do sit down," she replied. "Glad, did we set a place for Hilary? – we weren't, you know, expecting you till seven." Her mouth smiled slightly and her gaze stayed steady. I could not tell what she thought about my early arrival.

"I do hope it's all right that I've sugared it," Gladys said, bringing me over a cup of tea. "We're all sugar crazy here."

I was instantly alarmed: did this mean I was joining a very close, united group? I liked sugar myself, but what if I failed to conform over other, more important matters?

A tall young man with humour-crinkled eyes looked up from a pamphlet on mental deficiency he was scanning.

"Yes," he said. "In this unsavoury work we need all the sugar, sweetness, we can get." He turned slightly to return the gaze fixed on him by the spectacled girl the moment he stopped reading and added jovially yet cryptically, "Don't we Nell? She doesn't know what she's let herself in for does she?"

His condescending jocularity was irritating; however I responded with forced matching merriment:

"Oh dear, I hope it's not that bad. I hope I've not been taken in about what I've been let in for. Still, in for a penny in for a pound."

The young man looked non-committal, then, turning to Gladys, remarked:

"By the way Glad. did Charly Dale come for his shoes this afternoon? He's at last starting his new job tomorrow and I've promised him the shoes he needs for it."

They discussed this matter for a while, but although (perhaps because) the conversation would have been instructive I could not take it in just then. Instead (to prove my aptitude for first encounters) I engaged Nell in a lengthy, tedious conversation about train journeys, marvelling that she could apparently be interested in anything so dull – or was she really? Perhaps people doing this sort of work had to pretend to be interested in uninteresting subjects and keep asking questions. But if so why weren't they asking me, their new colleague, anything? If they weren't interested in me then they should be. So I re-routed the conversation on to foreign travel, thence on to the fact that I had visited Egypt and Albania, which Nell fortunately hadn't. This meant that in this one respect I was superior to her, who henceforward would be my superior at work.

Another girl entered the room, noisy and breathless over what she had just been doing, jettisoning remarks about the room in a random rush.

"We shall just have to do something about the Owens," she said. "I must tell Monica. They've none of them been to school for the past five days and the Education has been round and the Probation Officer arrived while I was there, but Mrs Owens was lying quite inert on her bed like before saying she was going to give up the ghost, and Eddy's out of work again…"

She continued for several minutes until Gladys broke in:

"Yes, and my Alan Dixon has been truanting again, and I'm sure it must be because of anxiety over his father carrying on with that coloured woman next door. Mrs Dixon's so insecure she's forever nagging at Alan. I must ask Monica if I ought to work more with Mr or Mrs Dixon."

The jocular young man rejoined:

"Watch it Glad. or he'll get emotionally involved over you, and you know how you'd like that!"

Gladys shrugged her shoulders and wrinkled her forehead.

"Oh well," she replied distantly.

Nell remained silent, looking down at her plate, until the

young man spoke, then raised her eyes and watched him.

To make up for not listening properly earlier I tried to now, but what Gladys and the other girl were saying was all very complicated. My mind kept wandering.

What are they saying? Anyway isn't it a bit soon for me to have to try and take all this in? I haven't really started yet. Tomorrow after I've met Monica and properly begun it will be different... Where's the sweatered young person? – I'm sure people must get emotionally involved over her...And the beef-steak-faced young man and his message – I should have given it to them. And as the sweatered young person isn't here I suppose I really ought to tell them how Mrs Green, not Charly Dale himself, hadn't come for the shoes – anyway not before three. This may for some reason be vital information.

But when I told them the young man just said casually:

"Oh yes, and the coat of course."

"And there was someone else who did come," I added, wondering how to describe the beef-steak-faced young man seeing I didn't even know his name. I couldn't, surely, describe him like that? – it would sound so rude and as though I were the sort of person who noticed only the flaws in others.

While I was trying to decide what to say the girl who had come in late turned and looked at me, and for the first time I felt I was actually being noticed. She had large eyes which seemed both to gaze into me and to try to see right around me, as though she wanted to understand everything about me; and I didn't mind. The look was not so much probing as a look of wondering and waiting. So, reassured, I was able to finish off:

"He was a biggish young man with a rather rosy face and brownish hair, and he asked me to say he'd be back tomorrow. But I'm sorry, I'm afraid I forgot to ask his name."

"That must have been George," the girl responded. "He did say something about coming round either today or tomorrow. He's one of our friends – a mechanic. We're always having burst pipes and fuses and so on and George comes round to fix them – not that we can't manage ourselves actually, but he just likes to come and help." She paused, then added, "Are you by any chance at all good at that sort of thing? It can be very useful when your Clients get into a jam."

10

Pleased to be asked a personal question at last, I replied:

"Well mending fuses and that isn't one of my strongest points – but I'm sure I can learn how if you show me." She smiled and nodded approvingly.

"By the way," Nell remarked, "I don't think you've been properly introduced have you? Hilary, this is Ann."

"And I'm Ben, you'll be fascinated to learn," the jocular young man announced.

Chapter 3

There was evidently no set time for breakfast: people just meandered in and out of the dining-room. Presently I was alone at the table, trying, not very successfully, to concentrate on the paper. Godfrey entered the room.

"So you're Hilary. We must shake hands as I'm a Probationer too," he said in a public-school voice. He came over and, smiling, shook my hand, then sat down opposite me. "I'm sorry," he went on, "I was not back until rather late yesterday, after you had disappeared upstairs. I'd have liked to be among the first to greet my new fellow-Probationer, only one of my families threw a bit of a crisis. They're apt to do this you'll find. Afterwards I felt like having the rest of the evening off and going out on the town. You'll probably often feel the same way I expect, especially at first."

I like him. As both of us are Probationers we'll probably have things in common and will discuss our work together. I must ask him about things. He's the sort of person, young man, that appeals to me – tall, nice voice and smile. Will we go out together sometimes? How does he spend his evenings when he's not working? – Pubs? The pictures? Dance-halls? - though if his tastes match his voice it'll probably be symphony concerts and the ballet.

Scraping a modicum of margarine onto his toast, he continued:

"I hope you can stand our frugal way of life here – this plain breakfast I mean and the dump we live in?" Although it was a question he went straight on, "We feel you see that sort of thing isn't terribly important. Living here as we do in this slum neighbourhood among all these poverty-stricken people it would be inconsistent if we had too much comfort – armchairs, rich food and so on."

He was staring straight at me through oblique, compressed eyes that looked as though they were often screwed up in puzzled preoccupation. I agreed with him – surely to live abstemiously on bread and marmalade in a barrack-like atmosphere was suitably dedicated for people doing such work.

"Ben feels absolutely the same," he added.

So do the others view the matter differently? Perhaps it's not such a united group after all. A relief in a way, still surely they should all be united?

"What's your opinion?" he asked. I felt flattered but hadn't time to devise a suitably reply as he continued: "I think, myself, there's a lot to be said for the old settlement idea – you know, people choosing to live in the slums. This must boost the morale of the local inhabitants, but it means the settlement workers must give up all redundant luxuries otherwise they can't really hope to become one with the people they've chosen to live among so can't really help them much."

Gladys entered the room and announced:

"Monica's here, Hilary, but she's got some urgent phone-calls to make so she's asked me to give you some things to read until she's ready to see you."

We left the dining-room and went down the olive-green passage past the room where Betty had been bumping things because it was good for her. Through a half-open door I noticed a puddle on the linoleum. Had a jar of paint water been knocked over? – no doubt painting too was good for Betty.

"Oh bother," Gladys remarked. "Clara's not done out the Quiet Room yet and she knows what the children's habits are."

So it's true – all I've heard about how dirty this sort of work can be and how unsqueamish I'll need to be. Good, I'm glad – or am I?

Another door opened and the sweatered young person appeared.

"Clara love, I wonder if you'd terribly mind – could you possibly manage to do the Quiet Room before anyone else comes? The Kellies were here with the usual results," Gladys said, her voice so creamy with courtesy that perhaps she was concealing considerable annoyance.

So the smart sweatered young person has to clean out the Quiet Room even when this has happened in it! Whatever else does she do?

As we were going upstairs I said to Gladys:

"Who was that?"

"Who love? – Oh Clara you mean," she replied. "Her real name's Clarabelle but she can't stand it so we all call her Clara."

Deciding a mild joke might not be out of place, I remarked:

"I suppose it isn't really all that odd having the same name as a Disney cow in this sort of neighbourhood – I mean a lot of much worse names must get shouted out round here." But I may have said the wrong thing; Gladys just looked blankly at me.

"This is the General Office," she stated, pausing on the threshold of a room on the second floor. "You've not seen it yet have you, love?"

The walls were pale khaki; the uncurtained window was sprayed all over with urban scurf. On one clouded pane was a clumsy sketch of a man in profile urinating. I followed Gladys over to a filing cabinet.

"This is where we keep all the case-papers," she explained. "This is how they go. City centre here, docks area there, suburbs there, and so on, all according to number. And within them, A's here, B's there etc. – all alphabetical you see…"

It's too complex for me. I hate systems – never can understand them…How was that drawing on the window done seeing the glass must be dirty and clouded on the outside? Who did it? Why hasn't it been rubbed off?

"Yes I see," I echoed. "All the families whose names begin with K living in locality 4 are kept halfway to the centre of Drawer 3."

Surely none of them did it?…It could have been one of the junior Clients who needs to bump things – Betty or one of those Kelly children. Surprising though that such children are allowed in the office.

Gladys handed me a file saying:

"Monica thinks it would be useful if you started reading up the Finnigans till she's ready to see you."

Ben, rummaging in the drawer of a yellowish piece of furniture

– an erstwhile washstand perhaps – ornamented with a dingy toy polar bear minus one ear, remarked:

"Starting her off on the Finnigans is she – they'll give her plenty of food for thought." He chuckled.

Does he ever stop bantering, or is it just something he does for the benefit of new, female colleagues?

For a while I was quite gripped by the Finnigans' story. They were forever doing appalling things: Mrs Finnigan had once tried to slit her throat; a young Finnigan had committed arson; Mr and Mrs Finnigan had decided at least four times to separate forever then changed their minds. Presently, however, I began to get bored and baffled by the complex, repetitive tale of woe, much of which, being hand-written, was barely legible. My mind wandered.

Why have I been told to read about this family? – just to teach me about the work, or are the Finnigans going to become my case?... Oh dear, I must re-read that bit. How disgraceful not to be able to concentrate on my very first day. And worrying about not concentrating is stopping me concentrating...

Looking at my watch I saw it was by now nearly half past eleven.

Surely on my first day they shouldn't leave me for hours on end with nothing to do except read about some family I may never even meet.

At last Nell, wearing a pallid mackintosh, came into the office and said:

"Monica says will you go down and see her now Hilary please."

Gladys looked up at me, for once not smiling. She had a distant expression, as though she did not actually see me but were envisaging my first encounter with Monica, seeing it as something momentous. Then, after a moment, noticing me studying her, she hastily smiled.

"Have a nice interview, love," she said.

Chapter 4

I paused outside Monica's office door wondering whether to knock. I decided to knock and enter simultaneously.

Although it was a sunny day the room was lit by a naked bulb – no doubt because the one small, grimy window looked out on to a sooty, blank wall. The dark brown wainscoting and furniture were chipped and battered. These walls too were khaki, and here and there the paint was cracked and curled out enticingly. There were scattered grey patches where fingers must have felt impelled to snap great flakes off.

Monica was a large, young-looking, middle-aged person. She was seated at her desk in a straight, frail, bedroom chair. Clara was standing at a very small table sorting through some papers.

"I think we can finish those after lunch, Clara," Monica said; and Clara, having patted the papers into a neat pile, left the room.

Is she her personal secretary then, or does she simply do every odd job that turns up?

Monica turned and smiled at me.

"How do you do, Hilary," she said. "I'm glad to meet you at last. I hope you don't feel I've been very discourteous in not seeing you before. Unfortunately some rather urgent matters cropped up requiring my attention." She spoke slowly and carefully, yet pleasantly, making me feel as though just then I were the only person who mattered.

First she asked me one or two personal questions. She sounded quite warm and friendly and even laughed slightly when I said something humorous. I felt relaxed, not at first aware that I was being penetratingly inspected. I did most of the talking, drawn out by her direct questions and such sympathetic echoing remarks as: "Yes, I understand" or, "It is often like that I think."

Presently, however, she switched to the role of Group Leader. Ceasing to smile, although still speaking in the slow, low tone (did it after all betoken warmth and understanding?), she said:

"And now, Hilary, I must tell you a little about the group here and the work we do and the part you will be expected to play – though I shall not tell you a great deal at this stage. It is usually wiser to find things out for oneself. There is no single way of seeing life, I think, Hilary, so were I to endeavour to tell you too many of my views about this work and the group here, while

they might be true for me they would not necessarily be for you."
She paused, looking ruminative. I wondered if I should respond,
however she went on, speaking still more slowly, "For you see,
we all regard life differently and indeed live it differently – all
have different gifts to offer. There is really no single truth, Hilary
– anyway, not in this sort of work. If you don't already know
this you will find out in time as your experience here grows.
Indeed, it is essential that you do find out; for it is only by
knowing this that you can ever really hope to help people."

I listened attentively – she sounded so solemn and full of
conviction.

"You will find," she continued, "that much of this work is
frustrating. You will look ahead and see little or no light. But
you will learn in time to see the small sparks of hope,
encouraging signs and developments. Then you will find the
work worthwhile; eventually, I hope, infinitely worthwhile." She
paused and looked at me expectantly.

"Yes, I'm sure I will," I responded. She studied me keenly for
an instant, then, speaking more briskly, changed the subject:

"And now about the group. At present there are six of us. You
make us seven. I, as you know, am the Group Leader. I shall be
having discussions with you about your work and progress; but
for a while you will be more or less assigned to one of the other
workers." I was relieved to hear this, but she added, "Not that
that means you will do nothing but accompany someone else
visiting. For no two workers ever form just the same kind of
relationship with their Clients. You will have your own way of
relating to them. It is there, I believe, potentially in all of us. But
merely to watch and copy another worker would prevent it from
developing."

*I'm glad she thinks I've got potentialities. But it's a pity
in a way she doesn't seem to consider the group a single-
minded, organic unit. It's one thing for us to be different,
but for us all to be separate...*

Monica then told me about the other group members. Gladys
and Ben had been at the Agency longest – for over three years,
Gladys having come just before Ben. Ann had been there a year
and a half; Nell less than a year. Monica herself, surprisingly,
was a relative newcomer.

"Godfrey," she rounded off, "has been with us just over a

month. He, like you, is a Probationer." She stopped and looked at me portentously.

"Yes, I see," I responded, wondering what her expression meant. Speaking even more slowly, enunciating each word with great precision, she resumed:

"And now, Hilary, I must explain what being a Probationer means. It means that after you have been here for a certain length of time – not necessarily a very long time – once it has become possible to evaluate your progress, we, that is myself and the other senior workers – not Probationers of course – review your work in order to decide whether it is best and wisest for you to continue with us, or whether you are not quite fitted for the work and would do better and feel happier in something else." She paused briefly, then in a hushed, almost religious tone, went on, "For this work is not for everyone. There seems little doubt that some people embark on it without fully realising what they have undertaken, who are therefore not as happy as they might be."

How happy ought I to feel, I wondered. Wasn't it my task to try to make others happy and to suffer somewhat in doing so? I hoped she would explain, but just then the dinner-bell rang, terminating the interview.

Chapter 5

Surrounded by all the others at the dinner-table, I suddenly felt shy of Monica. Surely I had just revealed too much of myself to her? She said nothing to me throughout the meal, although I suspected, sensed, that she was unobtrusively watching me, no doubt to observe how I behaved in a group. Consequently I spoke very little during the meal.

When it was over and we were leaving the dining-room she turned to Ann and said:

"Yes, that is a possible idea, Ann. I do think you might try that line. And if working on Eddy's relationship with his father and his possible identification with his psychopathic tendencies doesn't work then we'll just have to plan something else. How many things have we tried now? – help over budgeting and coping with the debts, rehousing, trying to stimulate more concern for the children…" She was looking at Ann, yet I felt this summary of work with Ann's family was really intended for me.

"Yes, but I do think there's been some progress," Ann replied.

"Well perhaps just a little," Monica conceded, then turned abruptly to me and said, "Hilary, I wonder whether you would mind seeing to Betty this afternoon." It was a courteously disguised command. Without explaining what this task involved, Monica went off to attend to doubtless more important matters. Her brevity had perhaps been deliberate: she was giving me an initiative test.

I went upstairs with the others, hoping one of them had overheard the command and would expand on it so that I didn't have feebly to seek advice; but no-one said anything for a few minutes. I meandered round the office feeling tired and dispirited.

I hate this drab patchy linoleum and the one-eared toy
polar bear and the sketch on the dirty window pane.

Presently Gladys noticed me and in a low, slightly conspiratorial tone asked:

"Well, how did it go love?" I looked at her perplexed and she added, "What did you think of her? Did she ask you heaps of terribly personal questions?"

Oh, she means my session with Monica. Why's she so
interested? She looks almost avid.

Before I could answer Nell cut in with surprising acerbity:

"Don't be an ass Glad. You know perfectly well Monica never asks a lot of questions. She's far too clever to do that."

"Oh yes," Ben followed. "Our Monica can find out absolutely all she wants to without ever asking a single question. She's only got to see how you twiddle your thumbs in an interview to know whether you had an affair with your big brother when you were six."

He sounds bitter as well as amused. Does he resent
Monica having this power? Did he himself ever make love
to a six-year-old sister?

"Talking of questions," I said, "I wonder if you'd mind answering one or two for me please? Monica has just asked me to see to Betty, only I'm not quite sure just exactly what she wants me to do – I mean, what time does she usually come?"

Surely a simple, precise question won't reveal just how

helpless I feel. And I may glean some other, more useful
information from their answer.

"Oh, so you've got Betty this afternoon," Ann responded, looking at me speculatively. "I hope she isn't like she was yesterday. She nearly sent poor Clara up the wall."

"She's really Nell's you see, and before that she was Kitty's," Gladys unhelpfully explained. "But Nell has to go out this afternoon, so I expect that's why Monica's asked you to have her today."

"Starting her off the hard way, isn't she," Ben remarked. Then Clara came into the office and announced:

"Hilary, Betty's here."

I hesitated for a moment before going downstairs.

Shall I take something with me? Going to see to a child who bumps things because it's good for her without taking anything with me is a bit like approaching an enemy line without a weapon, shield or white flag... What about taking the polar bear? – but no, perhaps not. They might think I believe all small children like innocently playing with teddy-bears and so on, which isn't true, or else that I've had next to no experience with them, which is true but I don't want them to know.

In the end I took nothing with me.

Chapter 6

Betty was sitting just inside the front door on the lopsided wooden chair which she was jerking viciously to and fro. I noticed she had a cast in her left eye.

"Hello Betty," I said cautiously. "I'm Hilary. I believe we saw each other yesterday when you were leaving the house with Clara."

Betty stopped jerking the chair and appeared to look at me suspiciously (although as she was cross-eyed it was hard to gauge her expression).

I must have said the wrong thing – or said it in the wrong way.

For a moment I studied her in silence.

Perhaps she's just suspicious of me because I'm a stranger. Or, being a child who bumps things she may be hostile. Or is she frightened? Children living in this neighbourhood, Clients of ours, are quite likely to be frightened of just about anything – especially if their mothers are prostitutes and fathers vicious alcoholics. Though she may just be scornful of me because I'm new here. Children are supposed to have a lot of intuition, so she may even realise I'm actually rather afraid of her.

Betty stopped looking at me and gazed expressionlessly ahead as she resumed jerking the chair.

Whatever can I say to her? What shall I do? Monica or one of them is bound to turn up any minute and find me not coping.

Then in an unexpectedly definite voice she said:

"My Mum's got red 'air."

How ridiculous. She's just a silly little girl whose mother probably hasn't got red hair at all.

"How nice," I replied. "One of my special friends has got red hair too. Red hair's very pretty I think." I hoped to start a conversation with her and thus establish rapport, but she continued to sit jerking in silence. I was about to suggest we went into the Quiet Room when she stated:

"She's got blood red 'air – all bloody like fire."

So after all she is a very interesting child – talking about blood and fire, and in connection with her mother too. She must be in a most unhealthy emotional state. I'll tell Nell, then with any luck she'll tell Monica who'll then realise I've got insight and know something about child psychology.

"Shall we go in the Quiet Room?" I wheedled. "Then you can show me all the things in there and what you most like to do because I'm new here and need someone to show me." But she made no response. Perhaps I had adopted the wrong tone.

I simply must get her in there before someone turns up. Shall I try taking her hand? Would this be wise with a stubborn child?

She started monotonously to croon:

"Bloody, bloody, bloody Mummy. Bloody, bloody, Mummy, bloody…"

I don't know – perhaps it's not very significant after all,
all this about blood. She's probably just being naughty –
though I mustn't let myself slip into ever thinking
children are naughty when really they're always
maladjusted or something clinical.

Clara came out of Monica's office. Catching sight of us by the door, she came over, gave Betty a slight shake and said sternly:

"Stop making that stupid noise, Betty, and get along into the Quiet Room like a good girl with Hilary who's going to look after you this afternoon." She grasped Betty's hand and led her off into the Quiet Room. I followed, abashed.

So firmness, even a degree of force, may be called for.
And perhaps the song is only a "silly noise" – I'd better
not mention it to Nell after all.

"Most of the toys are in the toy cupboard," Clara said. "It's locked. I'll get you the key." She left the room and I did not see her again till next morning.

As soon as she had gone Betty returned to the lopsided chair in the passage and resumed her jerking and crooning.

The best thing, I suppose, would be to take the chair into
the Quiet room, then she can sit jerking on it for the rest
of the afternoon if she likes. If bumping things is good for
her I dare say jerking things is too.

Trying to sound friendly but firm, I said:

"Well Betty, I think we'll take that chair into the Quiet Room, shall we, then we'll be out of everyone's way." But she paid no attention and just continued to sit crooning. The only thing to do, I decided, was to remove Betty and chair bodily. She was small and light so I was able, with difficulty, to pick up the chair with Betty still seated, apparently unperturbed, upon it, and stagger down the passage towards the Quiet Room.

Just then Godfrey came downstairs.

"My word," he exclaimed. "Monica has given you a heavy assignment on your first afternoon."

Cheered by his quizzical tone, I put the chair down and lied:

"We were just playing Armies and Battles, and I'm the Red Cross carrying Betty off on a stretcher."

Oh dear – is that the right sort of game to have been
playing with her?

"What a marvellous idea," he replied. "The very best thing to

21

do with young Betty I'm sure – get her thoroughly wounded on a battlefield!"

He stopped looking at me and appeared to be seeing through me and away beyond, his oblique eyes narrowing almost to slits. Ruminatively he resumed:

"Though I shouldn't wonder if we don't all get wounded in a war before long – judging by what I read in today's paper. And this time it won't just be soldiers on a battlefield but all of us, everyone." He paused briefly, then, looking at me again, added, "Do you think there's any way of preventing a third world war?"

I know world affairs are terribly important and I wish I knew more about them. Still, it's a bit hard just now to switch from Betty to something so different and difficult as world war. But he mustn't think me dull – that I don't care about anything except this unimportant, squalid little corner of the world, which anyway would be smashed like everything else in an atomic war.

Cautiously I responded:

"Well, I suppose it will all very largely depend on what Russia or China does – also of course U.N.O." Realising this might sound a bit vague and feeble, I quickly added, "I mean the United Nations as it stands isn't really very effective is it? It needs more power I think."

I need not have worried. He nodded approvingly. Perhaps all he wanted was a spring-board from which to expound his own theories for he instantly responded:

"Yes, I absolutely agree." He gripped the top bar of the back of the chair on which Betty was still sitting (surprisingly quietly, lost perhaps in some grisly fantasy world where bloody mothers were burnt alive). He seemed to have forgotten she existed as he leaned slightly forward over the chair, as though about to deliver a lecture.

He looks so intense – tense too, his whole strong body. I do so like tall men. And his knuckles are quite blanched by his grip on the chair – quite white. Though his nice wiry-haired arms are all tanned, positively leathery. I can just see him on a platform at some important radical meeting making a vehement speech.

"U.N.O. as it stands certainly is a dead letter. What the world needs is a genuine, democratically elected parliament of the nations – a world government in fact. And a real world police force with teeth in it. There should be worldwide, free elections –"

But his lecture was cut short by Ann's voice calling from out of sight by the back-door:

"Come on Godfrey. Do buck up. We'll never get round to the Owens and the MacMahons before tea unless we get going."

He relaxed his grip on the chair and straightened up, muttering a mild oath as he shoved back the boyish fringe that had flopped across his forehead when he leaned forward.

"Duty calls," he said. "I'm afraid I must go now. I've got to help Ann mend some of her Clients' furniture. We must continue the discussion some other time."

Chapter 7

When he had gone I picked up the chair and Betty again and staggered back into the Quiet Room.

But she didn't want to jerk the chair any more. She made straight for a broken toy cot containing a large, stained, semi-decapitated doll. Its face was squashed in and it exuded stuffing. No doubt it had been used for playing out bloody mother fantasies.

She undressed it vigorously, ignoring the few remaining buttons and tapes on its clothing.

"Silly Alice. Silly, naughty Alice," she muttered.

Once Alice was undressed and exposed in all her pathetically flaccid doll's nakedness, Betty threw the clothes into a corner and chucked the doll back into the cot face down. Then she went over to the window and stood looking out. After a moment or two she blew on the glass and drew something with her finger in the clouded patch.

Probably it was she who drew the urinating man on the General Office window. What game shall I suggest playing? I need the toycupboard key from Clara – but she's probably in with Monica. I'd better not disturb them.

All at once Betty, still staring out of the window, said:

"I'm going 'ome now." As she did not immediately turn round or move I had time to weigh up this announcement.

23

*I'm sure she's just being perverse. Still, what shall I do? I
don't even know why she comes here. Is it to bump things
because it's good for her or because her mother goes out
to work and there's no one to look after her at home? How
I'd love to simply let her go home. It would show I'm not
a tyrant. And making decisions for herself may even be
part of her treatment, so to forbid her to go would be
positively detrimental. Still, they seemed to say she's
definitely supposed to stay here all afternoon, in which
case if I give in and let her go they may think I'm lazy,
or weak – or don't like children.*

Luckily Betty changed her mind. Abruptly turning away from
the window, she marched over to the locked toy-cupboard and
tried fiercely to wrench it open.

"I want to play ludo", she announced.

Both relieved and surprised, I joined her at the cupboard in
order to make quite sure it really was locked.

"Let go, Betty," I ordered, my voice this time sufficiently
authoritative to make her obey. I gripped the handle and turned
it smartly, pulling it out towards me as I did so. The door sprang
open with a metallic snap. I had broken the lock – I would have
to confess I had to Monica.

Betty promptly started scrabbling about among the jumble of
objects crammed together higgledy-piggledy in the cupboard:
the dolls, grubby teddy-bears, disgorging jigsaw boxes, scraps
of chalk, dominoes and the like. She dragged practically
everything out of the cupboard and spilled it carelessly about
all over the floor. Eventually she unearthed a flat box with a split
lid, which she carried over to the table.

"Come on," she said. "Let's play. I'll be red. You can be blue."
*It's really the first thing she's said to me personally – the
first actual indication that she's aware of my existence.
I'd better make the most of it and leave tidying everything
up till after she's gone.*

I joined her at the table. She had tipped the ludo counters all
over it. Several had dropped on the floor, but she had not
bothered to pick them up.

*Shall I pick them up myself? If I don't she may be annoyed
and not want to play. I could make it seem as if I'm doing
her a favour then myself actually organize the game,*

24

which would show who's really in control.

"Betty," I said, "there are some counters on the floor." I stopped to pick them up saying, "What a careless girl you are! We can't have a game you know unless we have all the counters." To placate her I added, "Here are two or three of your red ones you'll be needing."

I noticed that although there was a dice-shaker there were no dice. Suddenly I felt weary. Not caring how Betty reacted I said:

"Where's the dice Betty? Go and find it."

Startled perhaps by my sharp tone, Betty looked up at me timidly. She descended from her chair and stood still beside it, now appearing bewildered.

Doesn't she know what a dice is? – poor child.

"Come along. Let's look for it together," I suggested, feeling all at once more relaxed, able even to take hold of Betty's dank, grimy hand quite casually as we went back to the cupboard. We rummaged around for some time but could find no dice. Eventually I said:

"Well we'll just have to see if we can't make one, won't we?" – for surely this would be a suitable form of Constructive Play? Monica might even come in and discover us at it.

Now Betty adopted a cajoling tone.

"Let's play ludo. Come on. Do let's play," she badgered, grasping my hand compellingly. Then she hurried over to the table and started carefully to arrange the counters. Once I was seated beside her she tried to flick her counters into the dice-shaker.

Her so-called ludo is really just tiddly-winks. We didn't need a dice at all.

So for a short while we played tiddly-winks. Now and then Betty made brief, uninteresting remarks such as, "It's your turn now." "Now it's mine." "You've got yours in." "I've got three in – no, four." I responded with equally dull comments.

Presently she stated:

"I want to draw now." Instead of sitting at the table to do so she stretched out prone on the floor. I squatted uncomfortably beside her, recollecting that this was a floor upon which generations of Kelly-like children had performed.

To my surprise Betty chose an ordinary lead pencil rather than a crayon. She immediately started to draw the flat side-view of a house, whose tiled roof appeared to surmount it as a vertical, checkered continuation of the wall.

"That's my 'ouse," she said, drawing with such vicious, jabbing pencil strokes that once or twice the lead point tore the paper. As it lay flat on the floor, partly on the linoleum and partly on bare wood, some of her pencil lines wobbled in accordance with the floor-board grain.

I'll explore her background by questioning her about the drawing.

"You live in a house like that, with six rooms, do you, Betty?" I asked.

"It's me Gran's 'ouse, an' it don't 'ave six rooms. It's got four with six windows," she replied scornfully.

I shifted my position on the floor, feeling both rebuked and a trifle irritated.

If it's just her Gran's house there's not much point in asking about it after all. Is she being perverse or has she simply forgotten what she just said? I suppose small children are apt to keep changing their minds.

"The roof looks a bit funny doesn't it?" I said. "Shouldn't the lines go sideways, more like this?" I sketched in the correction as I spoke. Betty glanced cursorily at the correction then started to draw an angular figure which, being buttoned down the middle and supported by thick, oblong, un-skirted legs, was presumably male.

"Who's that?" I tried again.

"No one," she replied, adding after a moment, "It's me Dad."

A drawing which became her Dad only as an afterthought was probably not very interesting or significant.

"Why not draw your mother for me?" I suggested, hoping for a tempestuous artistic outburst in red crayon. But she merely scribbled with a green crayon all over the man's coat.

"'E's got a green coat," she explained.

"Yes, but what about your mother though?" I persisted. I rose slightly from my cramped squatting position and knelt beside Betty.

"She's got red 'air," Betty responded; but she did not proceed to draw her mother.

Perhaps her refusal to do her mother is as significant as some gruesome picture of her being torn apart and burnt alive would have been.

"It's raining," she explained as, with a blunt yellow crayon, she made four or five hard, diagonal strokes (perceptible less by their colour than by the wide, shiny grooves the flat lead made in the paper) round the green-coated man.

I did not find this interesting.

"What's your favourite colour, Betty?" I asked.

"Yellow," she promptly replied.

Such an insipid colour surely can't be her favourite. I don't believe it. She just said the first thing that came into her head. I doubt if she's even got a favourite colour.

However, a moment later she started to scribble haphazardly all over the paper with the yellow crayon.

"Yellow, yellow, yellow," she sing-songed.

More than likely she did draw the urinating man on the General Office window. If so, yellow may actually be her favourite colour, or anyway emotionally significant to her.

She stopped scribbling and suddenly spat on the paper, then smeared the mingled saliva and yellow crayon powder in long looping lines all over it.

Yes, certainly there's some Freudian significance in all this – I must tell Nell.

Just then heavy footsteps resounded in the passage. Betty instantly scrambled to her feet and rushed out of the room shouting:

"George – it's George!"

I followed her. The passage was empty. I could hear her hurrying down the flight of stairs leading to the kitchen and went after her. I found her in the kitchen stuffing a currant bun into her mouth. She was digging her left hand into a dish of marmalade. I was both indignant and relieved – now at last I need not hesitate about what to do.

"Come away from there. Stop being so greedy and disgusting, you naughty girl," I said. "You know quite well you can't go sticking your dirty fingers in other people's marmalade." I gripped her hand hard, so angry that I scarcely noticed its repulsive stickiness. "We'll go straight upstairs," I said, and began to drag her towards the door.

"Let go! I shan't go!" Betty shouted. She struggled, screeched and tried to bite me. No doubt she had been saving all this up throughout the afternoon. I dragged her out of the kitchen and back up the stairs.

When, thoroughly scratched and bitten, I had at last got her to the top Monica emerged from her office. She paid no attention to me at first but focused on Betty, who stopped screeching and struggling the moment she saw her. In her usual even voice Monica said:

"Well, Betty, what is the matter?" Without waiting for an answer, she went on, "It's nearly tea-time, so I think, don't you, it is time you went home now." Glancing at me, she said, "Clara can take her today as you don't know where she lives, and it might be a little difficult for you while she is behaving like this, and until you have become a little more used to each other." She went back into her office.

Chapter 8

Ben looked across the tea-table at Ann and remarked:

"I gather from Clara there's a good picture on at the Gaumont this week." He smiled at her invitingly.

I watched Nell, who was sitting next to Ben. She was delivering fork-loads of corned beef salad to her mouth with great concentration. Seen from that angle, the highlights on her thick glasses more or less obliterated her eyes.

Glancing back at Ben, Ann replied:

"Yes, Mrs Owens told me it was worth seeing. I might go at the weekend if I've got time." She turned to Nell and added, "You'll be here on Saturday won't you Nell? Maybe we can go to it together?"

"Thanks, but I think I may be going away this weekend," she replied, still looking inscrutable.

"Oh, are you really love? You haven't put yourself on the 'out' list!" Gladys exclaimed merrily.

"No, well I'm not absolutely sure yet," Nell answered. "It all a bit depends." Although her expression was enigmatic her face was a hint pinker than usual.

"Depends on what love?" Gladys pursued. But Nell just replied:

"Well I'm still a bit uncertain." Re-routing the conversation, she added, "But it doesn't awfully matter about the list till Thursday anyway does it? – I mean that gives Clara plenty of time for the weekend shopping."

So she does the shopping too! Is there anything she doesn't do – except I suppose actual casework?... What are they really talking about? There's more to it, I'm sure, than just going to the pictures and weekends off.

Ben was not prepared to be diverted on to the dull topic of weekend shopping.

"My word, our Nell's a dark horse isn't she!" he bantered.. "All mysterious about her weekend. I bet it'll be a dirty one. I wonder who's the lucky chap – who is he Nell?"

This time Nell plainly blushed. Ann looked sternly at Ben and said:

"By the way, Ben, I wonder if you'd mind coming round with me to the Jacksons on Friday to help mend their window?"

Why's she trying to change the subject? Does she for some reason feel partly to blame for Nell's embarrassment? I don't believe Nell really has planned to go away for the weekend – she just wants an excuse for not going to the pictures with Ann. But why? Doesn't she like her? Maybe she's hoping Ben will ask her now Ann seems to have declined his invitation.

Ben looked back at Ann unabashed.

"Yes, I think I might just about manage to spare you a bit of time," he replied.

"It's not me you've to spare time for, love, but the Jacksons," Ann retorted. I had not heard her speak so tartly before.

Monica and Godfrey at the far end of the table were cut off from the rest of us by an empty chair or two. They did not appear to have been listening to the conversation – although of course Monica might have been, even though she seemed to be reading some document down on her lap as she bit without gusto into a thick slice of bread and marmalade.

Godfrey was eating mechanically, gazing straight ahead of him, evidently lost in thought.

How splendidly disciplined – to be able to be so buried in thought with all this chatter going on. He must be pondering about something really profound. Does he

ever think so deeply about people? Doing this work of
course he must. I wish he would about me.

Suddenly he turned to Monica and stated:

"The Pratts, you know, are really a classic case of mother-identification on the part of Ronny. He doesn't seem capable of playing with other boys but is always engaged in feminine activities like shopping or bathing the baby. He just can't seem to identify with the masculine role."

Is he really talking to Monica or simply expressing his
thoughts to the person he happens to be sitting next to?

"It's really an interesting example of Freud's theory on the aetiology of passive male homosexuality – don't you agree?"

Monica slowly raised her head. She looked irritated.

"It is very easy and convenient," she replied, speaking more briskly than usual, "to pigeon-hole one's Clients into categories. You need to be very cautious about this and have very definite evidence before deciding some Client has this or that tendency."

"Yes but…" Godfrey took her up.

I stopped listening and instead studied his bearing as the discussion continued.

I like how he's sitting with his arms stretched out on the
table. Obviously he doesn't care about unimportant
things like table-manners. He's clasping his hands so
tightly his knuckles are all blanched again. And the way
he's sitting, twisted right round from the hips, not caring
that he's turned his back on the others – I like that. It's as
though he feels he and she are the only two people in the
world just now – what they're saying the only thing that's
happening or counts. He must be the sort of person who
can give his whole self, his undivided attention, to the
matter in hand and person he's talking to –
enthusiastically too. I'm sure his enthusiasm is genuine
and deep, though perhaps he gets enthusiastic about a
lot of different things at different times. So possibly
nothing, no one, retains his entire interest and attention
for long. His friendliness to me may just be typical of how
he is with most other people. But I wish he'd consider me
someone special – I hope he will.

Monica, capable perhaps of observing objects perceived by none of the five senses and used to hearing the significant utterances people failed to make, must (even while apparently deep in conversation with Godfrey) have been aware of me sitting in silence watching them. Suddenly turning towards me, she asked:

"I wonder what your views are on dreams, Hilary? Do you think they provide useful material about the unconscious?" She looked keenly at me for a second then, to my relief, added, "Though I daresay your modern languages course never brought you much in touch with Freud or the analytical psychologists. Godfrey is our great exponent of all the various psychological theories."

Is she being sarcastic, or quizzically kindly to make up for being sharp with him before?

Realising with shame that I had not been listening to their conversation I felt at a loss. After a moment I replied carefully:

"No well, we did some philosophy in the literature part of the course. Though I have read a bit of Freud on my own – and Jung too."

Surely having read Jung will impress them?

Swinging round to face me, now oblivious of Monica and apparently aware only of me, Godfrey said:

"Yes but can one make a valid distinction between philosophy and psychology? They're two sides of the same coin. Freud's ideas are practically a religion. You have to believe them then they're true."

She's watching us closely and listening hard – waiting to hear what I have to say. She's not going to join in. She wants to observe us...I don't really agree but I don't want to argue with him. Still I suppose I've got to say something – she's obviously not going to.

"Well yes I agree with you in a way," I began gingerly (knowing it was wise to try to disarm one's opponent in advance with an initial expression of agreement), "about philosophy and psychology being in a way similar." I stopped, trying to think what to say next. I thought so hard that suddenly I forgot Monica, relaxed and was able to continue fairly easily, "I suppose you could say all philosophers and psychologists do in a way go barking up the same tree – and theologians. But it often turns out to be a bit of a holly tree, then they all start barking at each other."

Godfrey smiled vaguely. I recollected Monica and glanced

surreptitiously at her. Her expression was enigmatic. No doubt my attempted witticism had been very clumsy, silly.

"But I can't quite agree with you," I resumed, "about Freud being religious. Surely he was the reverse. You've only to read —"

"I didn't mean Freud himself was religious but…" Godfrey cut in. And for a while the discussion, carefully listened to by Monica, swung to and fro. The others were by now engrossed in a different conversation.

Presently Gladys said:

"It's a quarter to, Godfrey." He instantly swivelled round to look at the clock.

"My God, so it is!" he exclaimed. Without excusing himself, he abruptly rose from the table and, his tea unfinished, left the room.

I was disappointed. Where was he going, I wondered, but did not quite like to ask.

Chapter 9

After tea Monica went off to give a lecture about the Agency to the local Debating Society. As she was leaving she said:

"Sometime you shall come along with me, Hilary, but it would be wise first I think for you to find out for yourself how we work here."

"Oh bad luck, love," Gladys said after she had gone. "I thought she was going to take you with her. You'd have learnt so much. She's such a wonderful speaker."

Ben was lounging against the mantlepiece, hands in pockets, in what appeared to be a studied pose. He smiled benignly yet mockingly at the rest of us as we cleared away the tea things.

"So," he presently asked, "who's the lucky girl? Who's going to the pictures with Uncle Ben?"

I was surprised to find him looking at me. But I didn't want to go out with him: I didn't feel up to an evening of light banter.

"Isn't our new Probationer going to grant me the privilege of showing her the seamier sights of the city?" he went on, then promptly turning to Nell (who appeared to be very busy not noticing him as she stacked up plates) added, "I'm sure Nell can give me the best of references as a guide through the red light district."

"Oh sure," she replied without looking up.

"Well I must go and get on with my washing," Ann remarked, and left the room.

Ben looked expectantly at me.

"I'm a bit tired after my first day here," I apologised, "so I think I'd better stop in tonight. Thanks all the same."

He scrutinized me for a moment, then, turning back to Nell, said:

"Come on then. Buck up or we'll miss the first picture" – no doubt having all along meant her to accompany him.

"But I promised Ann I'd go with her on Saturday," Nell replied with surprising petulance.

"Oh let her go with one of her many boy-friends," he rejoined. *Is he jealous of Ann's boy-friends?...Nell and he both seem to have forgotten she said she was going away for the weekend...he's really a bit of a sadist.*

"You know I can't go to the pictures without a sympathetic ear to whisper in," he pursued; then, probably to increase her jealousy, added, "And Hilary says she's too tired to come with me – though I'm sure she will another time if I ask her." He looked at me flirtatiously, and Nell, sighing, said:

"Oh well, if you're such a baby you're afraid to go to a cowboy film on your own I suppose I'll have to go with you." And off they went together. I was sure she had never for a moment really considered declining his invitation.

After they had gone Gladys and I did the washing-up.

"I expect you must be wondering a bit about us all," she remarked with a slight, secret sort of smile.

She seems to be asking a question, yet I'm sure she actually wants to pour out all her own opinions of the others...It's nice to be able to see through people. Only I won't be obliging – I'll pretend I don't want to hear her views, don't quite understand what she's driving at.

"I suppose I'll find out about it all in time," I replied vaguely. But Gladys was not to be put off – which was rather a relief as really I did want to hear all about the others.

"Godfrey is a Probationer too you know. He's got all sorts of theories and good ideas and has read a lot," she began, speaking so kindly that I at once suspected she didn't actually think much of him. As she was clearly so eager to comment on her colleagues I hazarded a direct question:

"Is he good? – a good caseworker I mean?"

The bluntness of the question perhaps took her aback; as a seasoned caseworker she probably extracted information in more subtle ways. Realising, perhaps, that it didn't do to be too critical of a colleague to a mere newcomer, she replied cautiously:

"Godfrey has quite a way with people and lots and lots of them are very very fond of him – though of course he isn't always invariably terribly practical."

Is she the sort of person who can't easily admit to flaws in others? If so, is this a way of not facing up to flaws in herself?...After all I will try and draw her out about them all.

"Ben and Nell seem to get along well together, don't they?" I lied, and was quite surprised when Gladys, just now so cautious about Godfrey, immediately embarked on a long, mainly uncomplimentary, account of Ben and his relationships. She might be reticent about her colleagues' professional abilities but she clearly did not mind gossiping about their private affairs.

"Oh Ben, you don't want to pay too much attention to him," she began in her conspiratorial tone. "He's really quite a one with the girls – or thinks he is." As she continued her voice grew more animated and her eyes glittered.

Apparently Ben had chased almost all the girls in the group at one time or another, with more or less success. Having described with gusto a series of his affairs, Gladys commented:

"I suppose in fact really he must have some sort of fascination for women – sex appeal, you know."

Has she ever been taken with him herself? Perhaps she still is.

Sounding now more thoughtful and detached, as though Ben were a Client, she continued:

"It's interesting how generally he seems specially to pursue the, well, rather less obviously attractive girls – I mean girls who aren't just terribly pretty, you know – terrifically physically attractive. Take Nell for example. She's awfully nice and a very

very good worker indeed", (which surprised me) "but she is, well, quiet looking, if you know what I mean, and not absolutely exceedingly pretty – just like Kitty and Kay I was telling you about. And she isn't, of course, awfully vivacious. Yet he really does seem to have set his cap at her."

How odd – I thought it was Ann, not her, he was after.

"He's really gone much further with her than he ever did with Ann or any of the others." She paused; then, sounding conspiratorial again, resumed, "We have even wondered whether something might possibly come of it – though Monica is not quite sure this would be for the best."

Probably this is really her view, not Monica's. For surely Monica wouldn't air her views on such a matter, discuss one subordinate's personal affairs with another – unless, as Gladys is senior caseworker, she does sometimes single her out for special intimate chats and discussions. If so, Gladys may well identify very closely with her and model her views on hers. Can this be why she seems so exceptionally interested in how I, a new Probationer, am getting on with her?

"I thought, though, he seemed rather interested in Ann still," I remarked. "I mean, he seemed pretty keen on her going to the pictures with him just now, didn't he?"

Ought I, a mere newcomer, to contradict the senior caseworker?

"Oh yes, he's keen on Ann in his own way," she replied vaguely.

Now she wants to drop the subject. How provoking she is. First she says he used to be keen on Ann then that he still is – what is the situation? I'll force her to be clearer even if it does annoy her.

Rather peevishly I pursued:

"But I thought you said he wasn't after Ann any longer – I mean I got the impression from what you said earlier that it's now just Nell he's interested in – but perhaps I didn't quite follow you?"

"Well yes, love, I know the ins and outs of Ben's affairs are a bit confusing," she replied, making no attempt to straighten out her inconsistencies. I was infuriated – so infuriated that I was promptly ashamed of myself. What right had I to feel so cross with a friendly, even tempered person like Gladys?

After a brief pause she continued, now sounding a trifle sententious, senior caseworker instructing Probationer:

"You see I'm afraid Ben undoubtedly has got difficulties. His father died when he was quite small and his mother was, I believe, very possessive. He never had a father-figure to identify with, consequently has always been afraid of not quite living up to the male role – living up to expectations. So he has had to have endless girl-friends, sometimes several at a time, so as to prove to himself he really is as much of a man as anyone. Then I think" (and now the conspiratorial tone returned) "he's really all the time actually looking for a mother-figure, because of his own mother being so possessive; which may be why it doesn't really seem to matter to him if his girl-friends aren't, well, terribly pretty and so on." She stopped.

If she can sum up – wrap up – his personality so easily,
like a neat parcel, whatever's in store for me?

"Why – is his mother so plain then?" I asked. Not appearing to mind my facetious tone, she answered fully and seriously, speaking so slowly that she managed to make the statement sound profound and important:

"Well I don't really know, love, because actually you see his mother has never been here and he doesn't seem to have any photographs of her in his room." I was baffled. We dropped the subject.

When we had finished the washing-up she said that much though she would have liked to spend the rest of the evening with me she couldn't as Mary Dixon, a Client, was coming to do some cooking. I was impressed by her dedication – dealing with a Client at the end of a hard day's work. Would I ever be prepared to devote myself so tirelessly to the exacting task of "giving myself to others"?

Chapter 10

I returned to the dining-room and sat back in a knotty-intestined armchair, wondering whether to write a letter. I was sitting doing nothing, all at once comatose, almost peaceful, when Ann marched briskly into the room carrying a basinful of wet clothes. I quickly straightened up and scribbled at random on my writing-pad – Ann mustn't catch me sitting idle.

"I was just writing a letter," I said awkwardly, realising too late that the pointlessness of the remark had attracted Ann's attention. She put down the basin and regarded me searchingly. I was embarrassed.

"You look tired, Hilary," she said, clearly not deceived by the letter-writing ploy. "You must have had a terribly exhausting day". Since she could obviously tell how I was feeling and sounded sympathetic I relaxed, no longer needing to pretend, and responded:

"Yes, I suppose I am a bit tired."

"I know what it's like on your first day," Ann went on. "On mine I went to bed straight after tea and cried myself to sleep – I'm not sure why. Just the general strain, I suppose, and wondering what I was doing and what they were all doing and if I'd ever be able to stick it." I felt comforted.

"Yes, I suppose I'm feeling a bit like that," I said. "Anyway, rather exhausted." Needing further reassurance, I added, "You must all of you get pretty worn out after doing this job all day."

I hope it wasn't only on her first day that she felt exhausted. I'm bound to feel tired out by the end of the day for ages.

"I'm sure in time you won't feel so drained – once you've settled in and are enjoying the work," she replied.

But supposing I don't ever enjoy myself here? Will this mean I'm no good at the job? I never realised social workers were actually meant to enjoy their work. Enjoyment and dedication don't seem to match. They cancel each other out. I must ask Godfrey what he thinks.

Ann was consoling again:

"But really," she remarked, "I do think it was a bit much, giving you Betty your very first afternoon. I wonder what Monica was getting at. But you didn't do too badly considering."

How amazing! Surely I was hopeless? Anyway, how does
she know how I got on with Betty? They must have been
analysing my work and me in my absence. But when?
I've been turned into a thing, an object. Haven't I got
anything to say about it all myself? And what does she
mean about Monica assigning me Betty because she was
"getting at" something?

For a moment I hated Ann and decided to snub her by
responding:

"Oh no, I was absolutely hopeless. I couldn't do a thing with
her." I was so angry and full of hate that I felt a real person again,
not just an object for them to scrutinize and surmise about.

There are private recesses in my mind they'll never
manage to invade...I can feel all the grooves and
contours of my body again, like when I first arrived and
met them all. I'm me, my many selves, which I shall
deploy as and when I choose. However hard they try to
prize me open and categorize, re-arrange, my contents
they'll never be able to take away my right to be me,
myself, in whatever way I please. Poor Ann – she's not
me and will never be able to enter into me fully and
understand what it is to be Hilary.

"No, you weren't hopeless with her. I wouldn't say that at all,"
she replied. "Betty's a real handful."

Feeling I had just won a battle against them all, I responded:

"Yes, she is clearly quite a difficult child. I imagine you must
have had an extremely hard time with her to start with. Nell still
has a long way to go with her hasn't she? – it is Nell who works
with her isn't it?"

"Yes, Nell works with Betty," Ann replied slowly, looking
speculatively at me with a slightly troubled expression, puzzled
perhaps by my unexpectedly lofty tone. I was instantly ashamed
of my hatred. Disconcerted by her protracted gaze, I changed
the subject:

"I've just had an interesting chat with Gladys while we were
washing up. She was telling me all about the group and the
people who've been in it."

Ann stopped looking at me and started to drape a clothes-
horse.

"Yes, she's been in the group quite a time now," she replied.

"About three years. She can tell you a lot of interesting things because our methods have changed quite a bit since she first came. She can tell you – in fact she'd love to, it's one of her favourite subjects – all about the old days and the Old Gang. A real old gossip, our Glad, when she gets the chance." She paused and picked up a blouse that had slipped off the clothes-horse, then added, "Though mind you, it's not been easy for her, and really she's not done too badly considering."

Making amends now for just having been so uncomplimentary about her?

"She used to have half her Clients coming round every evening. We never had a moment's peace. But she's managed to change all that quite a bit now, even though having them all dependent on her seems to fulfil some deep-seated need of hers." She stopped.

"It must be difficult to change one's basic approach," I prompted. I was finding this interesting.

"Ben now," she obligingly resumed, "hasn't tried nearly so hard to. He's very rigid and I doubt if he's got it in him to change much."

Really? – does she bear him a grudge for some reason?

"Monica of course," she went on, "has had a lot to do with it as far as Glad is concerned. Glad positively falls over backwards to try and absorb and copy her methods. It's almost comic – though actually I suppose it's rather tragic."

The door-bell rang.

"That'll be my Mrs Owens," she said, and briskly left the room. *Oh, so her clients call in the evening too…She's as much of a gossip really as Gladys – and less bothered about criticizing the others. The main difference between them seems to be that her comments are more spontaneous and emotional than Gladys's. Gladys, with her avid look and hushed tone, seems to relish gossip because it's something one shares – something that brings you close to the person you're talking to. She needs to forge bonds.*

Chapter 11

Soon after breakfast next day Monica sent for me. She was in the middle of a telephone conversation when I arrived. Clara was typing. She glanced up briefly at me then got on with her work. I stood awkwardly on the threshold, trying to look composed. Monica replaced the telephone receiver and, ignoring me, immediately started to write something in a case-paper.

Hasn't she noticed me? Ought I to say something – announce myself – say, "here I am" or, "I believe you sent for me"? – only it would sound so silly.

Then turning to reach for a book she appeared to catch sight of me for the first time.

"Oh, good morning Hilary. Is there anything I can do for you? Were you wanting something?" she asked with a courteous smile.

But she sent for me. She surely can't have forgotten. She must have noticed me standing here waiting. Does she like to keep subordinates waiting in order to assert her authority? It may be a test. She's noting my reaction when in an awkward situation as this may indicate how I'm likely to behave in the other uncomfortable situations I'm bound to get in in the course of the work here. Anyway, I'm sure she loves testing people. Years ago she must have decided that her main interest and job in life was going to be Other People. Yet underneath her steady, slow, suave manner she's actually rather cruel.

"I was told – I got some message – that you wanted to see me," I answered.

"Oh yes, that's quite right, I did want to see you, Hilary," she replied. "I want to tell you what I have in mind for you to do today."

I'm just an object again – or rather a shadow, an item on her agenda, a character in the play of her imagining.

However, instead of immediately planning my day for me she commented on my doings the previous afternoon.

"It was a useful experience for you to take charge of Betty yesterday," she stated.

Now Betty's just an object – a training tool.

"I hope you didn't find it too difficult an undertaking on your first day?"

*She's well up in the pressure-points of conversation –
knows just how to find out what she wants to. She may
like people to be frank and truthful with her as it proves
her verbal tactics have worked. So shall I confess what a
difficult time I had with Betty? – though I don't want to.
Anyway, was I a total failure? I could counterbalance a
confession with comments about all those psychologically
significant things I observed.*

Perhaps the pause while I deliberated how to reply was sufficient
answer, for she went on:

"Betty is a very disturbed child, and it is hardly surprising you
found her a problem. I daresay you have not previously handled
children a great deal?"

*Why be so condescending? If she's trying to reassure me
it can only be to get me to pour out more about myself.
And must she be so clinical about Betty, calling her
"disturbed", not just unhappy and naughty?*

With a slight laugh I lied:

"Oh yes, I've had to cope with quite a few difficult kids in my
time, with problems ranging from long-division to father-
fixations." I paused. Monica said nothing so I continued, still more
flippantly, "But none of them were nearly as difficult to cope
with, I'm sure, as me. I should think I had, and probably still do
have, every problem under the sun, including father-complexes."

*That should cut the ground from under her feet – show
her I know what she's up to and can see through all her
subtle little ploys to manipulate and pump me. Now it's
her turn to feel silly and uncomfortable.*

But she just smiled tolerantly and said:

"Well, Hilary, I hope you aren't too problem-ridden to help
me over a family in difficulties whom I should be grateful if you
would visit for me today." I assented, mollified by her tone.
"They are," she continued, "a family who have only just moved
into a Corporation flat. Previously they lived in appalling
conditions. Their house was falling to bits and bug infested.
There were only two beds for the entire family, which consists
of Mr and Mrs Carter and their five children. Indeed, there may
even be six by now. Mrs Carter became exceedingly depressed.
They had huge debts, and Mr Carter never seemed to stick at
any job for long." She paused, looking pensive, her thoughts

perhaps focused on the Carters just then rather than on me.

"Yes I see," I said. She looked sharply at me and went on:

"Anyway, they were re-housed. And thanks to the work of a previous caseworker their general morale has risen, so we don't consider it necessary to visit them regularly any more. However, it is wise from time to time to go and see how they are getting on. And I thought it might be interesting and useful for you to go today."

Useful for them? Or for me as experience? Or for her as a means of finding out about my casework potentialities?

"Mrs Carter may well be pregnant again."

Oh dear, I know next to nothing about pregnancy.

"They are typical of many of the families we deal with. Also, to some extent, they are what we describe as a 'success case'. It might interest you to see what, in this work, constitutes success. They live at 15c Danbey Buildings. You can read their case-paper before you go."

She's telling me the interview is over, yet without telling me precisely what to do with the family. I must ask, even if it does show lack of initiative. It just mustn't be another Betty situation.

Nervously, scratching the side of my knee, I said:

"What should I – what would you like me to, well, do when I'm there? I mean, what would be best, wisest? Is there something useful – I mean specific – I might be able to do that they would want done and would be useful? Or anything in particular to look out for and find out?"

She stared hard at me for a moment, then, speaking very deliberately, said:

"The Carters, Hilary, as I said are a family we feel need visiting periodically as they still undoubtedly do have a great many problems. It is time someone went to see them again, and it would, I think, be useful if you went today. As I said, you can read their case-history for all the details then you will know precisely what you are to look for."

I did not believe her.

"Yes, all right, thank you," I replied. "I'll go this afternoon then. That will give me time to read up about them properly first."

"If I were you," she said, "I should go this morning. Mrs Carter is apt to go out in the afternoon."

Chapter 12

I returned to the General Office. I could afford to spend only about a quarter of an hour glancing through the Carter case-paper if I were to fit in the visit before dinner. When I asked Gladys the way to the Carters' she said vaguely:

"The Carters?" as though she had never heard of them.

"They live at 15c Danbey Buildings, only I don't know how to get there," I explained.

"Oh, the Paradise Grove Carters," she puzzlingly replied. "You can work out the route, love, from the map on the wall."

She sounded a shade reproving. Perhaps I shouldn't have asked such an elementary question. However, she went over to the map with me and showed me not only the complex route I would have to follow but also the still more complex method of working out the route. I caught myself starting not to listen.

At last I set off on one of the rusty, decrepit Agency bicycles. It was the first time I had been out since I had arrived. Autumn was approaching, and all at once the bright freshness of the morning dissipated my anxiety and depression: it was blown away by the breeze. I looked up at the sky, scattered with wafers of wind-flicked cloud against the blue, and felt cheerful. I didn't care whether I knew how to get to Danbey Buildings or not – I could always ask the way. I was good at casual encounters. Why should I not easily and swiftly reach the Carters', and, once there, forge an excellent relationship with the family? Why, no longer seemed to matter. As they were a "success case" surely I needn't feel unduly anxious about them. I would simply enjoy meeting them and take an objective interest in what I observed. I no longer cared what Monica or any of them thought about the way I conducted the interview. It didn't occur to me that this was just how I ought to be feeling.

As I bumped along narrow, cobbled streets the bicycle's skeleton rattled beneath me in a jubilant death-dance. With the breeze blowing in my face and sweeping back my hair, I felt almost as though I were boating briskly over a choppy sea, it didn't matter where. In the end I stopped to ask the way only twice.

I was interested in the neighbourhoods I rode through. Cornwall Street was grey and uniform, flanked by two interminable stretches of low, solid building. The houses, segments in these stretches, were differentiated from one another only by their dull coloured doors two steps up from the pavement. It was a dreary street, but was it actually squalid – a slum? It wasn't exactly dirty. And what made a place a slum? – dirt? over-crowding? age? decrepitude? Should social workers ever allow themselves to think of places as "slums"? – wasn't this too derogatory to the inhabitants?

Cornwall Street was deserted apart from an ancient woman in a shawl who looked like a peasant from central Europe. She was shuffling along with an immense, sheet-swathed bundle on her head. Perhaps she was going to the wash-house.

Presently I was in a busier thoroughfare whose drabness was alleviated by one or two shops. Some women in hair-curlers and bedroom-slippers were out shopping. There were also some school-age children. Were they playing truant? Were they Juvenile Delinquents? Perhaps it was not the nature of the streets and buildings that made certain neighbourhoods "slums" but the behaviour of the residents.

Then I was on a broader, more arterial road. Here and there along it were half-demolished buildings, looking, with their gay patterns of exposed wall-paper, rather like slices of fancy cake. Or were they more like carcases? Or bodies opened up for surgery? For a moment I was reminded of how Monica was trying to open me up and examine me, perhaps in order to operate on my personality.

Three boys were hurling loose bricks at jagged remnants of masonry, not, apparently, aiming at anything in particular. They were shouting at each other unintelligibly. Was it the strangeness of the local accent that made them unintelligible or were the children I would in future have to try to help and befriend going to be rather like animals? These boys didn't seem to be communicating with each other at all, but just making random noises, letting off steam. But I mustn't allow myself such negative thoughts. Social workers must always like and respect other people and not pass judgement on them however disagreeable and degraded they were – indeed the more disagreeable and degraded they were the more they must be liked and respected.

The road became more tortuous, the sky more blocked off, narrowed, by tall, closely packed buildings. They were drearier and shabbier than those in Cornwall Street. Some seemed to be crumbling away. They were mostly long and thin (were their inhabitants correspondingly tall and emaciated?). Some were even leaning over at a very slight angle, as though weary of standing alone and awaiting their turn to be demolished.

The road began to go up hill. At the top it widened. The cobbles were replaced by smooth tarmac, polished by the sky's breadth and brightness. For suddenly one side of the road was empty. Instead of buildings there was a clear vista: a great slope of green open space where once perhaps, before they were destroyed by bombs or city planners, regiments of tall, dismal buildings had stood crowded back to back. Now the space was empty but for one or two children kicking a ball and calling out faintly to one another in the distance. Furlongs away the grass faded and merged into a maze of streets and houses, misty and mauve in the distance – almost alluring. Seen from far off, you forgot that these blocks of building threaded with narrow roads and alleys must really be as blank and dreary as Cornwall Street. Away beyond them the softly pencilled horizon pointed up its myriad chimneys, domes, towers, cranes and steeples. The city spread pale and still before me. I could hardly believe that if my eyes became telescopes that could penetrate the shimmering film of distance I would see an ant-hill of activity: docks, shops, slums, factories, cathedrals, offices, all seething with people of every age, race, creed and profession.

As I paused to look at the view I suddenly wanted to compose a piece of music. The contrasts and contradictions of the scene suggested interesting counterpoint and tonal structure, solidity and balance, unexpected pauses and long diminuendos. Reluctantly I remounted my bicycle and continued on my way.

Chapter 13

Danbey Buildings was a collection of large, yellow brick blocks of Corporation flats, embellished incongruously with stucco imitation Tudor timbering, and netted with flimsy looking railed balconies. The buildings were not set in a rectangle around a court but stood at random at the corners of a confusing junction of back streets interspersed with vacant lots.

Finding No.15c was a problem for there were no lists of all the numbers in each building at the foot of each staircase. Furthermore I discovered that the ground-floor flats of one building were 37a, b and c; those of the next building, 51x, y and z; those of the next, 1, 2 and 3. There seemed to be no adults in sight to help me out.

There were some clusters of unprepossessing looking small children. A few were bare-foot; most wore torn clothes; the majority were patched at the knees and partially masked with grime. There was also a scattering of disgracefully neglected infants, squirming around or squatting on the ground, poking and delving into any available dirt. A couple of tiny boys were minus their knickerbockers.

As I stood surveying the scene a small van drove round one of the corners. The nearest group of children immediately stopped what they were doing. The back of the van was open. It was moving slowly and, as soon as it had gone just past them, three or four of the bigger children jumped up and flung themselves on the rear. They clung to the floor of the van as they swung their legs up behind them and tried to scramble in.

A couple let go almost at once and dropped back to the ground; another remained hanging on perilously; another two managed, like a pair of uncouth monkeys, to swarm nimbly up into the back of the van. One of them had a dark patch on the seat of his too-long grey shorts; the other's trouser seat was torn and the tattered tail of his grubby shirt spilled carelessly out and down over his belt.

A few moments after the van had gone round a corner the boy who had hung on behind reappeared. Then the van too reappeared on another of the roads that converged at the junction. One of the monkey-like boys jumped out of the back. The other, having quickly thrown two or three packets down to him, followed suit. They hurried past me into one of the buildings. I saw that their pockets were stuffed with bananas and bars of chocolate. The blue packets they were carrying looked suspiciously like bags of sugar and dried fruit.

Should I have just stood and watched? But what could I have

done? I didn't know where the boys lived, and the van had gone before I had fully taken in what had happened. I didn't want to get the boys into trouble, and if I reported the incident wouldn't I make myself thoroughly unpopular with all the flat residents, including the Carters?

A police constable walked round the corner. After inspecting the children he caught sight of me, came over and said:

"Excuse me Miss, but did you see two young lads just now? – about nine or ten they'd be."

How young and pink-faced and diffident he is – probably a new recruit to the force, unsure of himself – like me in a way....Anyhow, what a silly question. Standing here I'd have been bound to have seen lots of small boys.

"Yes, I've seen a great many little boys, all over the place," I replied. Still sounding irritatingly diffident, he went on:

"They'd have been carrying some packages of sugar and raisins and the like, Miss."

"Well most of the children are carrying something," I answered. "Whether or not any had packets of raisins and sugar I really couldn't say."

Why am I being so disobliging? – of course it's nice to feel in a slightly superior position after all those hours of being a raw subordinate at the Agency.

"They got them off of a van just now who's driver's just found out, and some people said as they'd noticed a couple of lads up on the back of it," he explained.

"There may have been a van," I replied. "Indeed there could well have been several."

"Well thank you, Miss," he responded, smiling. "Sorry to have troubled you. I daresay we'll find them yet."

I do believe he actually thought I was trying to be helpful! I suppose I needn't have been quite so stiff and unco-operative.

"I'm sure you must know this neighbourhood well," I said courteously. "I wonder, would you be kind enough to tell me how to find my way to Number 15c Danbey Buildings?"

Chapter 14

Directed by the young constable, I found Number 15c quite easily, even though it was at the far end of the top floor of one of the remoter Buildings.

On the way I passed one or two battered front-doors surmounted by panes of cracked or broken glass. Most of the doors were ajar or wide open and emitted depressing smells of cabbage and stale urine. Semi-clad, runny-nosed toddlers passed me on the stairs. In the distance I could hear the din of ranting mothers and bawling babies. I was appalled – at the same time intrigued.

The threshold of the Carters' flat was disappointingly different. The bright green front-door looked recently painted. The brass handle gleamed. The door looked hermetically sealed – perhaps the Carters liked to "keep themselves to themselves".

I knocked and was instantly filled with apprehension; I was about to make my first social casework visit. I strained to hear no approaching footsteps. If they were out I would have time to read up their case-paper and prepare myself properly for the visit.

I knocked again. There was still no answer, and I had just decided with relief to leave when I heard footsteps approaching the door – at least I thought they were approaching, but then (my dread mounting) they perversely veered off in another direction.

Someone was in. I couldn't very well leave. Should I knock again? They might not have heard me before; but if they had there was no point in knocking yet again – it might even annoy them. I did however, for I knew I would feel so ashamed if I returned to the Agency claiming no one had been at home when I knew they had been.

I even willed the approaching footsteps to maintain a direct scale towards the door. This time they did. The door opened and Mrs Carter (presumably) was standing there looking expressionlessly at me.

I was silent for a moment. I had failed to plan how to introduce myself. I noted vaguely that Mrs Carter appeared to be a moderately young woman who didn't quite match her impeccable front-door. Her finely plucked eyebrows rose a fraction and I found myself saying:

"Good morning Mrs Carter. I'm from the Hunter Street Agency. Monica – Miss Blake – asked me to call on you. I believe another Hunter Street worker used to visit you sometimes."

She smiled broadly at me. Moving aside so that she no longer blocked the entrance, she responded:

"Oh, you're from 'Unter Street. Long while since I saw any of you lot. 'Ow's Joyce an' Ben an' Gladys an' all getting along these days?"

Good – we're called by our Christian names. I'll feel more at ease so will probably do better being "Hilary" rather than "Miss Green".

"Gladys and Ben are fine," I answered, smiling back, glad that Mrs Carter seemed quite welcoming. "I don't know Joyce though. She's left and I've only just come you see."

Oh dear – I shouldn't have said that. She may be annoyed to find she's been fobbed off with a raw recruit.

But she continued to smile. Wagging her head slightly, she remarked:

"Ah, our Joyce – proper girl she was – proper lady. Did no end for us. Just about everything you might say. Got us this flat an' all, an' me away on me convalescence. Them was the days." She paused and looked ruminative.

Is she re-living a blissful past when everything was done for her? Whatever will she expect of me?

"There are six of us now you know," I remarked, "Monica, Gladys, Ann, Ben and Godfrey. My name's Hilary." (I forgot Nell.) "I expect you get to see quite a lot of different workers?"

I hope she does. I'd feel less weighed down and worried if we all partly shared our clients.

Without responding, Mrs Carter invited me in. As we walked down the passage she said:

"We've got the over-lay now for Willy's bed from the Assistance, but one o' the legs o' that Walton's cupboard's too short. Wobbles something terrible an' I shouldn't wonder if it didn't go an' fall right over one o' these days on top of our Kathy's 'ead. She will keep poking round an' sticking 'er fingers in everything. She's that wicked I'm sure she'll fall in the fire one o' these days. I'm sure I just don't know what to do with 'er – an' me with me 'aemorrhages an' all. An' our Willy an' 'is asthma's fair killing 'im, an' Mr Carter only just back in work an' no stamps in 'is book."

We were in a small, plank-floored room. The base of the wall was smeared and looked kicked. The only piece of furniture was a scratched, metal bed.

"That's it," Mrs Carter announced. I made a rapid mental resumé of her string of non-sequiturs and decided she must be referring to Willy's bed's new over-lay – whatever that was.

"That's good," I said, pushing my features into a suitable expression of mild admiration. "You must be delighted to be properly fixed up now."

How do you get over-lays from the N.A.B? Don't they just hand out money, not goods? However am I going to find out all this sort of thing – these essential administrative matters? Will Monica give me a briefing session sometime on the practical aspects of casework? Dare I ask the others? – It might be wisest to consult Godfrey. After all he is a fellow-Probationer.

Mrs Carter embarked on a series of remarks about the over-lay and how she had acquired it. I should have listened, but instead, while interjecting occasional encouraging comments, I allowed my mind to wander.

What's a Walton's cupboard? Is "Waltons" an old-fashioned word like "Tall-boy" for some special sort of chest or cupboard? – A local term maybe? Or is the member of the family who uses the cupboard called Walton? – that would be a rather grand name for one of the Carters. And its wobbliness? Could a big cupboard (and surely a Walton's one must be massive?) topple over if a mere child pushed it? A bit hard to visualize – this huge, lopsided cupboard, or whatever it is, crashing over after being poked by a tiny Kathy. But supposing it did actually fall on her head and injure her, what would happen seeing Mr Carter's got no stamps in his book? Doesn't a father have to have stamps for his child to get free medical treatment?...I know next to nothing about the ramifications of the health service either...And her haemorrhages – what does she mean? She looks too healthy to have TB. Should I press her for details then try to advise her? But I don't know how to. I don't know

50

*anything about haemorrhages, except for the natural
monthly business. Anyway, she's talking about
something else now. It might be difficult, awkward, to get
back on to the subject. Haemorrhages sound a rather
private sort of illness.*

Mrs Carter led me into another room where, although it was
a sunny day, a heavily banked up fire was smouldering.

"There it is," she said. She indicated a strange piece of furniture
sprouting irrelevant knobs. Its pseudo-antique surface was
chipped and cracked. It looked decidedly out of place beside
two modern, threadbare, square-armed chairs and a pair of
bedroom wooden ones on a stretch of tattered linoleum. Once
it may have been some sort of miniature sideboard, but by now
it had obviously acquired a different function. One of its open
doors revealed a clutter of underwear.

"Been like it ever since we bring it down from Walton's," Mrs
Carter continued. "An' 'Enry did go an' tell 'im as one of its legs
was broke, but Walton, 'e said couldn't be 'elped an' what's
bought's bought."

Annoyed with myself for not having guessed why it was a
Walton's cupboard but unable to suggest any remedy for the
wobbliness, I went over to it and pushed it gingerly, hoping to
appear businesslike and knowledgeable.

"Yes, it is wobbly isn't it," I remarked. Mrs Carter responded
crossly:

"Course it is. It's a proper shame going an' selling a thing like
that for all that money an' thinking folks like us'll put up with
it. I've a good mind to tell the police. It's always the same with
these coloured nigger people. Ignorant lot. Never able to get a
job in months, 'Enry – an' all on account o' them niggers. Makes
your blood boil. Didn't never ought to've been let leave their
own country's what 'Enry always says."

*It would be breaking casework rules to get into a
discussion about race…We sometimes help clients over
repairs. I read this in their case-paper and the
Finnigans'. And beef-steak-faced George is supposed to
be good at that sort of thing.*

"I'll tell the others about it," I said. "Then perhaps one of us –
one of the men probably – can come round and see to it."

"It don't matter," she replied disconcertingly. "Walton says as if we take it back up to 'im 'e'll fix it for us in a couple o' hours. 'E's that 'andy at fixing things. 'Bring it back Mrs Carter,' 'e says, 'an' I'll get it done for you inside a couple o' hours so's you'd never know the difference.'"

I was silenced by this switch from blame to praise of Walton and refusal of Agency help.

"Kathy, you wicked girl, don't you go doing that!" Mrs Carter abruptly exclaimed. Kathy was scrabbling amongst the overflowing contents of the Walton's cupboard.

Must she be so harsh? I should warn her about the danger of being too severe with one's children – though it might be a liberty to offer this sort of advice at this stage. And anyway social workers aren't supposed to lecture their clients.

"What's she doing?" I asked.

Perhaps it will dawn on her that she's being too severe with Kathy. If so, it may set the stage for a constructive discussion with her about Kathy's behaviour and her reactions to it.

"It's them sweets she's after," Mrs Carter explained. Kathy continued to rummage among the clothes, but Mrs Carter didn't seem to mind any more. "I always gets three pounds o' sweets Mondays to last the week," she continued. "'Enry, 'e's got a real sweet tooth. An' I 'ides 'em in there from the brats. It's them she's after." She paused and stared at Kathy; then, sounding faintly bored, said, "Now I'm telling you, Kathy." Addressing me again, she added proudly, "Little devil she is for anything sweet."

What does she mean? Doesn't she really mind Kathy's rummaging at all? Perhaps she thinks all mothers should shout at their children periodically whatever they're doing.

"Well you don't seem to have managed to hide them very well, do you," I remarked with a slight laugh. "She certainly knows where they are!"

Mrs Carter didn't seem to mind being teased.

"A real sweet tooth 'Enry 'as," she said. "Our Kathy, she takes after 'er Dad she do." She paused. I decided to make a few general remarks about sweets and sweet teeth, but she continued, "Before we was married 'e said to me, 'Mary,' 'e says, 'whatever kind of a cook you are always give me plenty o' sweets an' we'll always be 'appy.' Not, mind you, as we always 'ave been. There's been ups an' downs. But we always come back. We always do come back."

Too late I realised that her drift from sweets to life with Mr Carter might have informed me about her marital relationship (presumably the sort of information I should be gleaning). But not quick enough to switch on to her tangent, I said:

"Yes, I always like a few sweets myself after dinner. But they do put on weight so."

"A great sweet-eater Dad was," she followed. "A real big man. Like a pair o' them big red balloons in Woolworth's 'is cheeks was, only more brick coloured you might say."

What an amazing simile, coming from such a woman.

"I did get so into trouble with Joyce on account o' them sweets. Tuesday by Tuesday she'd come an', 'ave you gone an' spent all the Allowance on them sweets again,' she'd say. She'd say it nice, mind, but she'd say it. An' 't wasn't no use, 'cos I always did."

She doesn't sound a bit ashamed. She's quite proud of having withstood Joyce over at least this.

For a moment I forgot I was myself a Hunter Street caseworker in direct line of descent from Joyce; then I remembered and felt guilty. Projecting my self-reproach on to Mrs Carter I said:

"But do you really think it's awfully wise to spend quite so much on sweets? – I mean, sweets aren't very good for children's teeth are they? And surely you need all your money for proper food."

She crumpled up in humility. Sounding on the point of tears, she replied:

"Yes, 'opeless I am. I'm that soft I don't know 'ow to say no to 'em when they comes pesking me for sweets. Honest to God, I do try, but I just don't know 'ow."

Is she going to cry? If so, what shall I do? I've hardly ever seen a grown-up weep. I wouldn't know quite what to do with a crying child, never mind an adult. None of the casework textbooks I've read said anything about this. I'd like to get up and go. It's what I'd normally do rather than try and be comforting. But I suppose I can't very well, seeing I'm her caseworker. Should I ignore her crying and try to discuss something practical? Or should I try to console her? But how? – murmur sympathetically,

or touch her perhaps – a pat on the shoulder, or light
touch on the forearm, or an arm across her shoulder?
But whatever I do she's bound to tell it's forced and be
resentful, not comforted.

The front door slammed and someone came running down
the passage. A thin boy of about nine in long grey shorts entered
the room breathlessly. He was carrying a couple of blue paper
packets and his eyes were shining excitedly, almost hectically,
in his lean, pale face.

"I've got 'em Mum," he said abruptly. Then he noticed me and
stopped short. An expression of rapidly obliterated recognition
appeared and disappeared on his face. He looked faintly familiar
so I said:

"I've seen you somewhere haven't I?" Immediately, I realised
he was one of the van raiders.

As soon as Mrs Carter heard him approaching she looked
tensely expectant. Now she adopted an expression of
surreptitious entreaty as, in false surprise, she said:

"Why Willy, I thought you'd 'a' been back 'alf an hour ago.
Go an' get all that dirt washed off o' your 'ands an' face."

His face is quite clean.

"An' don't you never let me catch you coming in 'ere again
looking like that."

Awkward situation. I'm out of luck. She seems to be trying
to keep us apart. Yet she's showing me what a scrupulous
mother she is, with all the right ideas about cleanliness
– the sort of mother whose son couldn't possibly be a
Juvenile Delinquent.

Willy obeyed and promptly left the room. Leaning slightly
towards me, Mrs Carter said in a woman-to-woman tone:

"Full day's work ain't it love, keeping 'em clean?"

Is she trying to curry favour by conferring honorary
motherhood on me?

"An' our Willy's always out busy at something an' dirtying
'imself something terrible. That busy 'e always is at something
or another. But then, they can only be young once can't they?"

I didn't know what to do.

"Yes, children are bound to get dirty," I conceded, hoping to
reassure her thus encourage her to continue prattling about
inconsequential matters. I needed time in which to decide what

line to take over Willy. Mrs Carter chattered nervously on about children always being children.

Shall I tell her what he's done? Should I try and advise her about how to deal with the business? – though that might be too direct and bossy. I must try and be subtle – help her to see for herself why he behaved as he did and work out her own solution…But of course she probably does know what he did. She may well even have got him to do it, in which case I'd better not say anything. I mustn't ruin my chances of forming a good relationship with my very first client – frighten her in any way, even make her hate me. Should I consult Monica before doing anything? A mere Probationer surely can't be expected instantly to deal single-handed with such a difficult situation but should be allowed to put off making any decision about such a grave matter? I'd better leave.

I glanced obviously at my watch and interrupted Mrs Carter's monologue:

"Certainly prices are going up and up these days. It's all one can do to buy enough clothes to stand up in." Infusing my voice with appropriate sympathy, I added, "It must be much worse for you with all your big family to buy clothes for."

Ignoring my terminating tone, she replied:

"That it is. An' our Albert, 'e's that set on getting all them expensive, la-di-dah, tight-fitting Tedwardian clothes. Spends all 'is money on 'em. An 'Enry, 'e says…"

As she rambled on I strove to think of a polite way of ending the interview. I glanced at my watch again, even more obviously, and, trying to sound suitably reluctant, said:

"Yes, well, talking of food," (for by then we were on to the costliness of tinned peaches) "I see it's nearly lunch-time, so I'm afraid I just must go now. Mustn't keep them waiting!"

"But you 'aven't 'ad your cup o' tea yet," she responded, and left the room before I had time to decline the offer. I felt thoroughly annoyed with both of us.

Presently she reappeared with a large cup of heavily brewed tea, all slopped down the side and into the saucer. The chipped rim and crack in the china probably seethed with bacteria. I scalded my mouth as I tried to sip the over-sweet liquid too fast.

"Thanks so much. That was lovely," I lied, setting the cup

down. "But I really must be off now."

Mrs Carter accompanied me down the passage. At the front-door she stopped and faced me. In an extremely confidential, Gladys-like tone she said:

"It's these 'aemhorrages you see, love, as is bothering me. They leave me all weak and wasted away feeling you might say. An' 'Enry, 'e says…"

If only she'd raised such an important matter earlier instead of going on and on about unimportant things like the price of tinned peaches. I've done my day's work with the Carters now. I shan't listen any more.

"I'm ever so sorry you're having all this trouble," I said. "I'll let Monica know and see if she has any suggestions. And I'll tell one of the men about the cupboard and ask one of them to come round and fix it."

She thanked me and I returned to the Agency.

Chapter 15

After dinner I stood about in the General Office wondering whether Monica would summon me for a discussion about the Carters. Gladys and Nell were seated at the table writing; Godfrey was pacing to and fro talking about the inadequacies of local government welfare officers' training. At last, sounding ultra-pleasant, Gladys remarked:

"But Godfrey, love, you've not had much social work training either, have you?"

He looked surprised, then said:

"No, I suppose not. Still, as a Probationer here I'm surely getting the best possible training aren't I?"

I'm in love with him. He's so tall and striking. And he's got such wide interests. I'm kind of in league with him. Gladys has no right to mock him. And it's so loveable – his constant perplexity, as well as his detachment. Almost makes me feel sort of motherly. Perhaps he'll find out I'm the only one who understands.

He turned abruptly towards me and, to my delight, said:

"Are you doing anything this evening, Hilary? If not, would

you care to spend it with me?"

"Yes, I'd love to," I at once replied, quickly suppressing the thought that the invitation might merely be a way of withdrawing from the others.

"Great," he said. "We'll have a splendid time." He stuffed some case-papers into his attaché-case and left the room.

"Did you see that?" Nell asked, and Gladys replied:

"Yes, I know, love. But what can you do?"

What is it? What's wrong? Oh I see, he's broken casework rules: taken his case-papers out with him. He's a devil – not orthodox, bound by petty rules. How shall I defend him? – I mustn't be tactless.

However, the talk wandered off on to other topics, then they resumed their writing. I felt bored and cross and presently asked if they would like some help, but they replied vaguely and went on with their work.

I drifted dully over to the misted window and stared down at the hot, rather flabby scene. The morning breeze had died down. The lean, slightly lopsided buildings opposite were only wanly shadowed in the dusty sunlight of the drained out afternoon. I decided to read some case-papers – anyone's.

After about half an hour Nell put on her pallid mackintosh and left. Gladys wound a sheet of paper vigorously into a vintage typewriter and started laboriously to tap out a stacatto letter. I was infused with tepid dreariness. The sound was a little like the intermittent buzzing of a blue-bottle against a window pane. Gladys grimaced slightly as her clumsy fingers pounded and plodded over the keys. I awaited the pauses and prestos of her performance and could not concentrate on my reading. Then winding out the paper with a sudden rush, she said:

"How would you like to come and visit the Kellies with me?"

"I'd love to. Thanks very much," I replied, agreeably surprised by the abrupt invitation.

On the way Gladys told me about the family. They were about forty pounds in debt. They owed considerable sums to their landlord, the gas company, a neighbour (probably an unofficial money-lender), a pawnbroker (to whom they had relinquished a suit and most of their bed-clothes) and a hire-purchase furniture firm (from whom they had obtained three beds and a long since removed, glossy, shoddy dining-room suite). Their gas meter had been broken into four times – probably by themselves, although this could not be proved. The two eldest sons were in an approved school for stealing barley sugar from Woolworths eighteen months ago. And Mr Kelly, who had been in prison twice himself, was apt to beat up his wife, enjoyed beating his sons and, it was suspected, abused some of his daughters in a less acceptable fashion.

"And so you see, love," Gladys concluded, "they have to compensate for their father's aggression by stealing and so on."

"What about the girls?" I asked.

If they don't steal barley sugar how do they compensate for their paternal mistreatment?

"Well I'm trying to work with Eva especially," she replied. "We got her into a club, but that didn't work; they said she was one of the 'unclubable'. And the Child Guidance gave her up because they couldn't get anywhere with Mr and Mrs Kelly. So now I'm concentrating on her myself. We chose some material and I'm helping her make herself a dress. She drops in quite often at other times too, when things get too bad at home."

She's saying all this with positive relish. It bears out what Ann said about her. I believe she actually wants her clients to keep visiting her. It must fulfil some deep, personal need. Her life may really be rather empty so she has to live vicariously. That could be why she's a gossip too.

"The younger children come to play in the Quiet Room sometimes don't they?" I remarked, hoping my good memory would impress her.

"Yes they do," she replied, sounding a trifle surprised. "Usually when their Dad is home and getting tough. But they haven't been since you arrived have they?"

"No, but I overheard you saying something to Clara about their having been," I replied.

"Oh, did I?" she said, speaking slowly and looking at me thoughtfully, rather as Ann might have done.

Reassured by this minor success, I felt quite self-confident by the time we reached the Kellies, prepared to relax and watch Gladys at work almost as though I were at the theatre.

Chapter 16

The Kellies' home was just as a Client's should be. Gladys knocked on the rotten front-door that years ago may have been bright blue but now was drab navy.

"Anyone in?" she called out. Not waiting for an answer, we went straight into the living-room.

It was more like a cave than a room. Two panes of the single small window had been replaced by squares of brown paper. Entered from the sunshine outside, the room seemed even darker than it would have been anyway. It took me a few moments to become acclimatized to the dimness. Then I noticed that the walls were mottled, streaked and bumpy, in places actually crumbling away. In the gloom they resembled the rugged, multi-toned sides of a cavern.

And the room's occupants seemed rather like cave-dwellers. One or two filthy, semi-clad toddlers were wriggling about on the tattered, puddled linoleum. A heavily slumped forward woman in a shawl was seated in the remains of a padded armchair. She was so still that she and the chair appeared to be united. Sitting beside the coal fire (whose shifting light and shadow pattern contributed to the cave-like effect), she resembled a witch: at any moment she might lean forward and stir a bubbling cauldron. At the same time she was primitively massive – a Henry Moore sculpture.

Two lines of washing hung from wall to wall – perhaps partly responsible for the puddles on the floor. The dangling garments, suspended like stalactites, flickering and ghostly in the firelight, looked like the garish festoonery for some savage festival.

Gladys flopped into a dingy, unwholesome sofa which caved in at the centre.

"Well, Mrs Kelly, how are things going?" she asked cheerfully.
I'd rather perch on the arm. It may be threadbare and grubby but who knows what vermin may not be lurking in the murky, cushioned depths and litter-crammed crevices. But if I don't relax on the sofa like Gladys, she and Mrs Kelly may guess how I'm feeling. I'll just have to get used to this sort of thing.

Gingerly I made myself follow Gladys's example and tried to forget about the obnoxious insect-life probably seething amid

59

the cushions beneath me.

"Terrible, Gladys duck, something terrible," the shawled woman replied with a deep sigh.

For a few minutes there was silence apart from the infants' scrabbling noises.

Is this initial pause deliberate – part of her interviewing technique? She surely hasn't got stage-fright because I'm here.

Presently, in a guttural, expressionless tone, Mrs Kelly continued:

"'E's gone off again. Gone on one o' them jaunts of 'is."

Slightly bowing her head, Gladys, in a low, ultra-comforting tone, responded:

"Oh I'm so sorry. You must be feeling very very upset."

If she isn't she'll feel quite guilty… What sort of jaunts does she mean? Drinking bouts? Spells in jail?

One of the infants knocked a jam-jar containing a couple of bedraggled marigolds off the up-turned grocer's box on which it was precariously balanced.

"Billy, now look what you've gone an' done. Don't you never let me catch you doing that again," Mrs Kelly said loudly yet indifferently. She rose from her chair. Standing up she looked frailer, less monolithic and witch-like, although now obviously pregnant. She slapped the offending child perfunctorily on the bare buttocks then deposited him like a defaulting puppy in another corner. Without bothering to clear up the mess on the floor, she returned to her chair and relapsed into silence.

"Look Billy," Gladys said to the child, now crouching in a sullen, punished attitude, as though he felt like a whipped puppy. "I've got a new, many-coloured pencil here. Come and see."

He approached her cautiously. Despite his griminess, runny nose and bare (possibly also runny) bottom, she picked him up and set him as deftly on her knee as if she had been his mother.

Will I ever be able to dandle filthy children like that?

Gladys produced a four-colour silver pencil and, after briefly demonstrating its mechanism, gave it to Billy to play with.

The front-door opened and a girl of about five ran in, a packet of sliced bread under her arm. She too was grubby, but being curly-haired and pink-cheeked and wearing a fairly fresh looking cotton frock, appeared more wholesome than the other children.

"'Ere it is, 'ere it is, but 'e says not next time till we've paid up," she said excitedly.

So they're in debt to a shop too – a typical casework problem I suppose. Interesting to see how Gladys deals with it.

Gladys did not, however, respond, nor did Mrs Kelly look abashed.

Have they got beyond the point where they need to discuss such superficial, mundane things as bread bills?

Mrs Kelly took the packet and dropped it limply on the floor by her chair. It landed in a puddle.

"Go an' find Ron," she said flatly, sounding as though she didn't care whether or not she were obeyed and didn't expect to be anyway.

The girl stared at me.

"'Oo's that?" she demanded.

"That's Hilary, Mary," Gladys replied. "She's a new Hunter Street lady."

It's the nearest she's got to introducing me since we arrived.

Still ignoring me, Mrs Kelly asked:

"'Ow's Kay getting on these days?"

"She's married now and going to have a baby in a couple of months," Gladys replied.

"Oh my!" Mrs Kelly responded, and there followed a long, dull conversation about Kay and other members of Agency, past and present.

Why don't they talk about something interesting, important, like Mr Kelly's jauntings and his treatment of the children – especially the girls? Does Gladys always start off by gossiping about trivialities? Perhaps she really is inhibited by my presence.

Mary disappeared through a door at the back of the room for a few minutes. When she returned she settled on the floor at my feet. She leaned her head back against my knees and moved it slowly to and fro.

Is it itching or is she inviting me to pet her? I wish she wouldn't – she's sure to have lice. Still, I suppose it's a sort of compliment. At least someone's noticing me. I'd better

*stop just sitting here doing nothing. If I don't respond at
all to her Gladys is bound to notice and think I can't form
relationships with children. But if I manage to play with
her maybe she'll be impressed.*

I leaned forward and tentatively fingered Mary's neck, which
instantly squirmed this way and that for a second or two then
turned a delighted chuckling face towards me. Encouraged, I
hoisted her on to my lap, for a moment forgetting her grubbiness
and the Kelly children's reputed habits. She may have been used
to sitting on social workers' laps for she immediately started to
fiddle with my collar, undoing then doing up again the top two
buttons of my blouse.

*Her little pink finger-nails are black rimmed. There's that
waft of poor-children-smell. Shall I put her back on the
floor? – But no, perhaps not. This is a good opportunity
for showing I can relate to children.*

As I didn't know what to say to Mary herself I said to Mrs Kelly:
"What a pretty little girl."

"She's pretty enough," she replied gloomily. "'Er Dad's little
pet's what she is."

*Can she be jealous of her? I suppose she might be if what
Gladys said about how he behaves towards his daughters
is true.*

"She looks like you though," I lied. I was rewarded: Mrs Kelly's
morose expression broke into a beam of pleasure as she turned
to Gladys and exclaimed:

"Well I'll be buggered! First time I ever did 'ear my pretty little
Mary looks like 'er old Mum! But she don't look so like 'im, do
she?" She guffawed. Gladys smiled non-commitally and Mrs
Kelly repeated hilariously, "No, our Mary don't look so like my
Ned, she don't!"

*What's so funny? What does she mean?…Oh, perhaps Mr
Kelly isn't actually Mary's father. A pity I said anything
about her appearance.*

Mary scrambled down from my lap and hurried across to a
cupboard in the corner of the room. Half hiding behind it, she
wheedled:

"You can't see me. You can't see me now." The invitation was
too pressing to refuse.

"I wonder where Mary's gone," I responded, rising reluctantly from the sofa and following her over to the cupboard.

"You can't see me. You can't see me can you?" Mary screamed excitedly as I approached.

"Be quiet you," Mrs Kelly remarked placidly in her direction. Turning back to Gladys, she explained:

"It's all them boils and that tonic Dr Brown give 'er's making 'er this way. I don't know what's gone an' got into 'er since 'e give it 'er. She didn't never used to be this way, always carrying on over something." For a while she and Gladys talked desultorily about nothing in particular.

"I'm coming after you, Mary," I said with mock ferocity. "I'm a lion." I was about to add that I was going to gobble her up when I realised that this might be frightening for a child who was a Client. So I abruptly changed the nature of the game.

"You're a monkey, Mary," I said. "A little red monkey at the zoo, and I'm giving you a banana through the bars of your cage."

I'm managing to play with her quite successfully – I don't care what I do. Never mind the puddles on the floor and the horridness of touching other people's mouths – especially the mouth of a little girl who almost certainly never cleans her teeth.

I knelt down, stretched my arms behind the cupboard and offered her my forefinger as a banana. She grabbed hold of it and sucked it vigorously.

Good. She's enjoying the game. All the same she's sucking very hard...Mr Kelly and his daughters?...

I abruptly withdrew my finger; however, Mary called out excitedly to the others:

"Look. Oh do look. I'm eating a banana an' I'm a little red monkey at the zoo." They didn't stop talking to look at her so she repeated shrilly, "Look at me Gladys. Look at me Mum. I'm a little red monkey in a cage with a banana."

"Oh yes, so you are," Gladys replied, and Mrs Kelly, regarding her balefully, remarked:

"Don't know I'm sure about no bananas. Can't afford nothing like that. But you're a monkey right enough. There's times I wish" (and she turned back to Gladys) "as they was all in cages – an' 'im too. They're more than I can do with, honest to God they are. An' another on the way. I keeps saying to 'im, 'Ned,' I says, 'I ain't going to 'ave no more I ain't.' But it don't make no difference, 'e's that ignorant. Back 'e'll come after one o' them jauntings of 'is, an' right after me 'e'll be. Ain't no use trying, is it?"

Just then the door opened and a short, swarthy man walked in. With bristly jowl and shaggy, matted hair, he too looked a suitable occupant of this cave-like dwelling. He crossed the room and went straight out through the back-door without taking any notice of us.

When he had disappeared Mrs Kelly for the first time properly acknowledged my presence. Leaning towards me, cupping her hand round her mouth and slightly turning and nodding towards the back-door, she said in a loud, melodramatic whisper:

"That's 'im."

"Got me tea ready then?" he shouted from behind the door, which he had left ajar. It opened into a back-yard. I could hear a tap running.

"Give us time for Chrise sake, Ned," Mrs Kelly shouted back, then remarked, "That's 'im that is, that's 'im all over. Always shouting for something. If it ain't 'is tea it's 'is coat as is gone over the road anyways, an' 'oo's to blame for that's what I'd like to know? – what with all 'is jauntings an' boozing."

I wondered why his coat was constantly over the road, but then Gladys remarked:

"Oh yes, that reminds me. How about the blankets? Did you manage to get them out again after I saw you last time?" Presumably "over the road" meant in the pawn shop.

"Well, yes an' no, Gladys duck. You see it's this way –" Mrs Kelly started off, but her prevarication was cut short by Mr Kelly re-entering the room. He seated himself heavily on a fragile looking wooden chair and demanded:

"Well, where's me tea?"

"There you are. What did I tell you?" Mrs Kelly said triumphantly, but Mr Kelly, turning to Gladys, grumbled:

"You'd 'a' thought she might 'ave got me tea ready when I've been out 'ard at work all day earning 'er every penny we've got in the world. But there 'tis. Women's all the same."

They both seem to be treating Gladys and me as a court
of appeal – because we're social workers?

"Lot o' pennies we've got, an' a long time you've been back in work!" Mrs Kelly retorted.

Then Mary, who had previously, unnoticed, left the room, re-entered. She made straight for Mr Kelly, who snatched her up and held he on his knee.

"It's me Mary!" he exclaimed.

I watched closely as father (or anyway adoptive father) and daughter focused their attention on each other; she seated astride his apart planted legs, the skirt of her short dress pulled well up her thighs, facing him and fiddling with his dirty open shirt collar; he saying endearingly:

"Well, if it ain't Mary. 'Ow's me little pretty today?" He placed his leathery, grimy paw quite far up her small white thigh and patted it gently.

I glanced at Mrs Kelly to see how she was taking this; but she was merely looking down as she drew her shawl about her before rising from her chair. She withdrew to prepare the tea.

"So the landlord's got the tap fixed at last," Gladys remarked. "I had quite a job persuading him to get it done. Do you know," she went on, turning to me, "for weeks the Kellies haven't been able to wash properly because the landlord wouldn't mend their broken tap in the yard."

Did they really mind? – they look dingy enough even with the tap working.

"It's all them Capitalists," Mr Kelly announced. "If we 'ad a Communist government now, things'd be different. All these 'ere good-for-nothing landlords'd all be likidated, that's what they'd be, every one of 'em."

"Mr Kelly is a real red Communist," Gladys explained.

I decided that, having forged a good relationship with Mary, it was time I showed I could with an adult member of the family too. So I said to Mr Kelly:

"Do you think, then, that all the workers of the world should unite and overthrow the Government by force as Karl Marx and Engels said?"

He glared at me and rejoined:

"'Twasn't no Karl Marx said that as I've 'eard of. That's what us Communists going to do. An' we're hathiests, not angels."

"Yes well," I pursued, "that's what you think is it? – I mean that all workers should band together and try and overthrow the Government?"

Glowering at me, he replied fiercely:

"That's what anyone's got an ounce o' sense in 'is 'ead knows'll 'appen. Like they done in Russia an' China, where they killed all o' them old blood-suckers off an' now everyone's got all the money 'e wants an' can live decent with televisions an' fridges an' electric blankets – not," he went on, growing more excited and declamatory, forgetting to pat or clasp Mary as he accompanied his speech with Latin-style gestures, "in an 'ouse like this 'ere – if you'd call it an 'ouse – with a roof's what's falling in, an' rain as comes in, an' a tap as don't never work, an' a back-yard where all the tom-cats in town comes a-yowling an' don't never let a chap sleep in peace –"

Mrs Kelly turned round from laying the table and remarked to me:

"It ain't them cats as keeps folks awake. It's 'im with 'is you-know-what – talk about tom-cats! – an' then all 'is snoring. It's them tonsils of 'is. I keeps telling 'im, but 'e won't 'ave 'em out."

"'Ave 'em out!" he bawled at her. "What, me lay down on a white table-cloth an' let them nobs put me to sleep then like as not cut me throat for me while I can't do nothing about it – me as ought to be out an' slitting all o' their throats!"

But I shouldn't be getting into a political debate. That's not casework. Casework's supposed to be digging, burrowing, into your clients' souls – or rather, their emotional lives. Probing that goes no further than asking questions about taps and blankets is mere furrowing on the soul's top-soil, unlikely to help your clients to resolve their deep-rooted conflicts – and he seems to be raging conflict personified. Nor is it likely to plant seeds that might one day blossom and transform their personalities…Should I try to make good Gladys's omissions, even though she may think me presumptuous and interfering?

"You feel pretty strongly about fighting and getting rid of authority figures do you?" I asked. "People with power I mean."

That surely can't have been a too probing, personal question? It may stimulate him into some useful self-examination. And it will show Gladys I'm aware of the significance of aggressive feelings towards authority figures.

"Power's all right," he replied. "I like to see a fine powerful chap meself. I always was a one for the wrestling."

"Yes, an' we don't never get to pay the rent every time you go to it," Mrs Kelly rejoined.

"I didn't mean that sort of power – body strength," I persisted. "I meant people in power over you – the boss – you know, people like that."

Casework must be hard enough even at the best of times – a difficult, delicate operation. But with such unintelligent clients as these, who don't even seem to talk the same language as reasonably educated people, it's surely an almost impossible task.

"I just told you what ought to be done to the bosses, didn't I? – they ought all to be likidated," Mr Kelly chided.

Here's this uneducated, probably unintelligent, even perhaps subnormal man, a mere client, in effect accusing me, a social worker with a university degree, of stupidity! Still, I won't give up.

"Yes I know," I answered. "That's what you, as a Communist, naturally of course feel about landlords and foremen and managers and rulers and –"

"Never said nothing about no foremen," he broke in. "'Ad some quite decent ones in me time. Used to go 'ome after work Thursdays with one of 'em. An' 'e'd lend me 'alf a dollar every time I was broke an' we passed the 'Lion'."

"No, well not foremen then," I continued doggedly.

Would any foreman ever have dreamt of accompanying him home, much less lending him money?

"But what I mean is, do you find you nearly always hate people who are over you and tell you what to do?"

Exasperatingly he replied:

"No one never told me what to do in me life."

I'll be rash. I'll risk asking a more fundamental question, never mind the possible immediate or long-term consequences. I'm sick of his irrelevant responses to my more general questions. Anyway, he deserves to have to try and answer a more personal, probing question.

"What about your father?" I hazarded. "Did you, when you were little, hate having to do what he told you and even feel like murdering him sometimes?" I looked searchingly at him. But all at once he lost interest in the conversation and returned his attention to Mary, fingering her curls and patting her thigh again.

67

"'E never 'ad no father," Mrs Kelly explained. "An' more's the pity. 'Twould've done 'im a power o' good. Many's the time I've said to 'im, 'Ned,' I says, "Twould 'a' done you a world o' good to've 'ad a dad. Made a different man o' you.'"

This uninteresting dénouement to the debate made me feel rather flat and foolish, so I was relieved when Gladys glanced at her watch, then, heaving herself up from the sofa, said:

"Well, it's time for our tea too now. I'll look in again early next week."

We returned to the Agency.

Chapter 17

"Well," said Gladys as we were walking along, "What do you think of them?" After a slight pause I answered:

"Mary's quite a bright little thing, isn't she?" Gladys agreed.

"Yes," she said, "it often surprises me that she's such an attractive child, coming from a home like that. Though mind you, she's not always so attractive. She gets terrible temper tantrums, and Mrs Kelly doesn't know what to do except more or less have a tantrum herself. Mary's got these pretty frocks, compared with the others', because Mr Kelly actually goes off to the market after getting his pay or dole – before he's boozed it all – and buys them for her. He doesn't bother about getting her underclothes though, so she's not quite so pretty underneath."

I've simply no idea how to cope with clients' crises.

"What do you do about the temper tantrums?" I asked. "Is there any advice you can give Mrs Kelly about them? – or shouldn't one ever give advice exactly?"

"Well, love," she replied. "It's not just a question of Mary, you see. It's the problem of the whole family. We are a family agency, you know, and try to help the family as a whole."

I know. She doesn't need to tell me that. But she obviously does, must, know a lot – much more than me of course. She's a skilled, experienced caseworker. Still, I must pursue this point and get her to stop generalising and be more precise about how to tackle temper tantrums.

Gladys changed the subject.

"Talking of Mary," she remarked, "She seemed really to take to you."

I was surprised and encouraged by the compliment even though Gladys at once diluted it by adding, "But of course she is a generally bright child – not usually at all shy."

I must get her to tell me just what the family's situation is and what we've done for them so far – fill out on what she told me before.

"How is it Mary's so friendly and extroverted with a home like that?" I enquired.

I must make up for my lame response when she first asked what I made of the family.

"I mean with parents so in conflict, and living in such squalor, I daresay not getting enough to eat, and a mother who nags so, I'd have expected her to be, well, quieter and more withdrawn."

"Yes, it is more what you might have expected," Gladys agreed. "Though of course she is very wilful."

Good. I'm glad she agrees. But is she impressed by my insight about Mary? She's more baffling than I thought at first. Is her general friendliness and good humour, her seeming vagueness and woolliness, in fact a cover for alarmingly acute powers of perception and a capacity for deft personality manipulation? She is, after all, senior Caseworker, and has, apparently, absorbed a great deal from Monica.

"Anyway," she added, "she certainly did seem to take to you. You had a fine game together – and Mrs Kelly was pleased too. She obviously quite took to you as well."

How could she have? – I hardly said a word to her the whole time. Perhaps she's just trying to avoid mentioning my unfortunate conversation with Mr Kelly – my breaking rules by getting into a political debate with him. She may in fact be quite annoyed that I took it upon myself to try and probe one of her clients' deeper feelings. In any case, as she clearly doesn't much like criticizing and reproving people she probably wants to steer clear of the subject of my discussion with Mr Kelly. All the same, it's nice to be complimented, even if the compliment isn't deserved. I'll ask her a few more questions.

"How do you actually work with such a family?" I said. "I mean, just what specific kind of things can one do? And in this case of the Kellies, has it been possible to do much? Are they in fact much different from when you first started with them?"

I instantly regretted this last, perhaps somewhat tactless, question; but Gladys did not try to answer the questions individually. Her reply was once again frustratingly blurred and general.

"Yes, you are right, it is difficult," she said. "The main thing is to get the right relationship with the family as a whole. The rest follows gradually you will find." Perhaps my final question had struck home, for she continued a trifle defensively, "But of course such families progress only in very small stages. To anyone but a trained caseworker, in fact, no progress at all might be apparent." I felt rebuked. "It is very difficult to say just how you work with this family or that," she concluded, "as they are all different and you simply can't generalise."

Chapter 18

It was Group Discussion Evening – Pallaver Night as Ben termed it. Godfrey must have forgotten when earlier on he had invited me out.

After the tea had been cleared away we re-seated ourselves round the table in order to discuss one or two of the more problem-ridden Clients and "any matter of domestic concern anyone may care to raise", as Monica put it. We would, she added for my benefit, be discussing these matters "as a group".

So are we a group only when seated consciously – artificially? – round the table for the express purpose of discussing? And why isn't she sitting at the head of the table as she does at meal-times? Is it because this is an occasion when we're all supposed to be equal, hierarchy forgotten? Anyway, she's at the top end of one of the sides – as near the top as she can get without actually being there.

Everyone was present except Godfrey.

"I wonder where Godfrey is," Monica said. "I think perhaps we should wait two or three minutes until he comes down."

She sounds non-committal, yet I'm sure she's really annoyed. Probably she makes a point of concealing her feelings – except occasionally when for some reason she deliberately reveals them or even conjures them up.

"I think he's upstairs writing a letter to *The Times*," Nell remarked.

"Oh is he," Monica replied. She paused, then, turning to me, resumed, "We meet like this, Hilary, every two weeks as we feel it is advisable for all of us, as individuals, from time to time to bring to the attention of the whole group any problems we may feel have arisen, either as regards our work or with respect to everyday domestic matters."

It's like being an adolescent in a primitive tribe getting initiated into its rights and customs.

"Yes I see," I replied politely.

Is she telling the truth? Is that really why we have these meetings? Probably not. I expect it's mainly because she enjoys conducting businesslike proceedings and dislikes the group's usual casualness. Now and again she may like to – feel she ought to – enforce a little dignity and decorum.

We waited a moment or two for Godfrey, then Monica said:

"Well I think perhaps we should begin now." She asked if anyone had a problem to raise. Since no one apparently had, she continued, "This is an appropriate moment, I think, for welcoming our new member. Hilary, we hope you will be very happy here with us."

"Yes, love, we do hope you will be," Gladys echoed in a barely audible murmur.

She intended all along to start off by formally welcoming me. It doesn't sound spontaneous – more like the first point on a mental agenda. She may know from past experience that no one is likely to be able instantly to think of one of the many problems they want to raise so there's bound to be a moment's silence. I daresay she likes there to be an initial short silence. And she wouldn't want to be the first one to pose a problem – that wouldn't be good group leadership. She's sure to be well up in all the group dynamics gimmicks and know that leaders must never lead but should draw others out. She may

71

even find trying to efface herself in a way pleasantly challenging.

I nodded slightly in acknowledgement and in a low hurried tone replied: "Thank you very much. I'm sure I shall be." No one spoke.

How embarrassing – they expect me to say something more, but what? They're waiting. I just must add something, anything.

"Yes," I said emphatically, "I'm certain I shall be very happy indeed here."

Why did I go and repeat myself like that? Now they're bound to guess how uncertain I really am whether I'm going to be happy here. And caseworkers are supposed to be happy and problem-free – Monica said so.

Then I made matters worse by adding, "This is such very valuable work, and helping people solve their problems must be most satisfying."

How pompous and fatuous! I shouldn't have let on, even hinted, that I need to feel dedicated and do good. Social workers must on no account want to do good.

Still no one said anything, which probably denoted general disapproval. After a brief pause Ann said:

"Yes, well there is something I want to raise. It's the lavatory seat. It's a disgrace. Something simply must be done about it."

"Yes," Gladys agreed. "It's certainly dreadfully cracked and difficult to clean properly.

"We ought to get a modern plastic seat," Nell stated. "It would be far more hygenic than our old wooden one. And plastic seats aren't dear. We could get one at Bingham's quite cheaply. I saw some there the other day."

Surprising – I'd have expected her to be a cautious discussion-follower, not a proposer of swift solutions.

But Monica evidently didn't want a quick solution; she wanted a full group discussion.

"Yes, I noticed some there too," she said. Looking questioningly round at us all, she added, "What do you all feel we should do about the matter? How important is it?"

She's expressing no opinion herself – probably because of her present self-effacing, discussion-promoting role.

"Well," said Ben, for once sounding serious, "I'm not

absolutely sure it is." He leaned a trifle forward and bent his face down, as though what he was saying were profoundly important, almost religious. "For do we really need a new lavatory seat? The one we've got serves its purpose doesn't it? And I don't myself feel it is right to go spending a lot on things that aren't absolute necessities."

"That is undoubtedly true, Ben," Monica appeared to agree. "The question perhaps is, what is and what is not absolutely necessary?"

Can't she say what she thinks about it? Is she going to stay aloof throughout the meeting? If so, it must be because she enjoys extracting other people's opinions while withholding her own as this gives her a sense of power. And it may help to remind her that even though she has deliberately effaced herself it's still she who really controls the meeting…Or has she actually got any definite views on this subject? – probably she'd be in favour of getting a new lavatory seat…I can see her now, planted on a lavatory seat, her broad buttocks slightly overlapping it, knees well apart, knickers down below tautly stretched skirt…I mustn't laugh…But it does help me to get my own back on her, seeing her like this…after all she's just an ordinary human being like the rest of us who has to wash and go to the lavatory and so on. But somehow she looks sillier than other people would, sitting there in the lavatory – I suppose because she's usually so decorous, ponderous. I feel quite powerful, even god-like, being able to see the Group Leader like this doing something so private and undignified – me, a mere Probationer.

Ann said trenchantly:

"Well I think it's high time we did at least have a decent lavatory seat, whatever else we do or don't have." She enlarged on this theme for a few moments; meanwhile my vision of Monica faded and my attention returned to what was being said.

Why's Ann being so forceful, positively severe? Is all this really very important? Maybe it's some thin end of a wedge. Very likely they're forever debating the pros and cons of making life as comfortable as possible here. Or is she unwittingly displaying antagonism towards Ben by opposing him?

"Yes I suppose germs and so on can accumulate in the cracks," Gladys contributed (like Monica, appearing to agree at first). "But there are other things to consider. It's really a question of priorities. We do really need quite a lot of things, some of them pretty expensive. I mean there's the linoleum for the General Office and curtains almost everywhere. And we ought really to get a pressure-cooker, the way we carry on over our meals."

"It is, indeed, as you say, Gladys, a question of priorities," Monica assented; and she looked across the table straight at her. She was not scrutinizing her but smiling at her widely with her whole face. For a moment she looked no older than anyone else in the room.

It's the first genuine, total smile I've seen her give. Before, she's only smiled with separate parts of her face – eyes and forehead or lips and jaw; and the smiles have always looked forced, false. But this one seems sincere, personal, even intimate – as though she's saying something personal and private to Gladys – rewarding her perhaps for echoing and enlarging on what she herself said…At the same time it's as if she's subtly trying to convey some very nebulous message to her – hinting at some tenuous bond between them, and veering towards some relationship neither of them are fully aware of and have never before so frankly acknowledged.

Gladys looked back at Monica seriously, raising her eyebrows a fraction so that her forehead was a trifle crinkled.

She feels humble. Her slightly supercilious expression may be an involuntary protest against her extreme gratification over being smiled at like this by Monica.

Then she slightly inclined her head, perhaps so pleased that she was embarrassed and unable to go on looking at Monica. But Monica continued to smile at her, and she started to doodle clumsily on the piece of paper in front of her.

"Yes, well if it's a question of priorities," Ben said, "I'd say buying more clothes and blankets and things for our Clients was far more important than just getting something to make ourselves a bit more comfortable."

I only half-listened.

I can see her on the lavatory seat again, only this time somehow it's not me but Gladys who's seeing her. Does she ever see, imagine, scenes like this?

Godfrey entered the room looking preoccupied. He sat down at the table without apologising for being late. Monica did not accuse him of unpunctuality, but, speaking even more slowly and deliberately than usual, painstakingly explained:

"Godfrey, we were just discussing the question of what we, as a group, need to have here at the Agency. Ann has just raised the question of buying a new lavatory seat, and we have all been carefully considering whether we would be justified in making this replacement."

He at once looked keenly interested and replied so promptly that this might have been the very matter he had just been writing about to *The Times*:

"Yes, this whole question of whether or not we should buy things that would make our own little lives here a bit more comfortable is of vital importance. The question in fact is: what are necessities – and what are our priorities? I think myself that what we may regard as necessities for ourselves might constitute luxuries for those living about us, to whom we should surely be setting a good example."

He sounds very certain – though he's generalising as usual, not dealing with the precise subject under discussion. And I don't really agree. Even dedicated caseworkers shouldn't be so ascetic that they're positively unpractical or unhygienic. A new plastic lavatory seat wouldn't be a luxury. And even though, as he says, we're supposed to be setting a good example to the poor families in the neighbourhood, that surely doesn't mean we should sink to their level? We should be encouraging them to have higher standards. But I won't say so. As a newcomer I oughtn't to join in this discussion. Anyway, I don't want to disagree with him.

"Yes, Godfrey," Monica replied, "I am sure we all do wish to set an example to the people round about us. But do you really think the best way of doing so is by letting our own standards slip?"

She sounds severe – punishing him for his unpunctuality? Annoyed because he's able to join in the discussion immediately without for an instant being at a loss for words?

Chapter 19

Presently Monica said:

"Well I think now we have all perhaps cleared our minds sufficiently about some of the issues raised by this question." She was evidently paving the way for someone else to conclude the debate, but no one spoke. By now everybody seemed paralysed with confusion.

> *Does she want us to vote? – probably not. Being so devious*
> *I expect she'd rather we reached a more nebulous group*
> *concensus – one leaving loopholes through which she*
> *can later unobtrusively percolate her own ideas.*

As the silence persisted she was forced to close the discussion herself.

"Well then," she said, "shall we leave it that you, Ann, check up for certain on what a new plastic seat would actually cost? – then we shall be in a better position to decide whether or not we would really be justified in buying one."

> *She's forgotten Nell's already found out about prices.*

"Yes, all right," Ann agreed. "Do you think we could next talk about Betty? It's high time we attempted some assessment of our work with her."

Monica assented, then, probably not wanting Ann to take over as topic-introducer and definer, continued:

"Also, I think it is important that we don't only evaluate her actual progress but in addition try to consider the effect of her visits upon us ourselves, the group as a whole."

"Yes, perhaps we should attempt to decide on the limits to which she should be allowed to go," Gladys contributed. "I mean we ought to try and work out more clearly than we have in the past just what she should and shouldn't be allowed to do when she's here."

> *How alarmingly often the words "try" and "attempt"*
> *seem to crop up. Does it mean we can never hope to*
> *actually succeed?*

Monica nodded approval at Gladys, who appeared not to notice. Then Nell countered:

"Well I don't know, but I'd always thought the whole point of the programme with Betty was that, because of her repressed feelings and cramping home life, she should have no limits set to her activities when she comes here."

*Does she resent the others commenting on her client, thus
in a sense on her as caseworker?*

"No limits set to her activities!" Ben rejoined. "Good Lord, my
dear Nell, would you honestly have her going through all the
jewel cases in your dressing-table drawers and letting off
repressed steam by setting fire to the kitchen curtains?"

Ignoring him and looking straight at Nell, Godfrey said:

"I'm inclined to agree with you: the Clients and their needs
must always come first. A disturbed, neurotic, perhaps even
psychotic child like Betty –"

"Oh come off it Godfrey old chap," Ben broke in. "Let's be
simple and just call her maladjusted."

"Very well then, maladjusted," Godfrey acquiesced. "Anyway,
a child of this sort, if she's ever to become emotionally stable
must surely have any and every opportunity, while she's here,
to work through her hidden conflicts, which means she must
have unbounded freedom of expression."

There was a brisk exchange about this for a while. Nell insisted
that Betty should have complete freedom – at the same time
agreeing that she should not be allowed to smash the Agency
windows. Ben supported her. Godfrey kept trying to start a
debate on unstable children in general, while Gladys strove to
keep their attention focused on Betty herself. Only Ann actually
discussed: asked people's opinions and appeared to be
influenced by them. Monica sat back and listened, occasionally
giving slight nods. Presently she leaned forward, looked hard at
me and said:

"I wonder what you, Hilary, as an unbiased newcomer, think
about all this? Have you any fresh ideas that might help? You
may have formed some opinions about Betty after your
afternoon with her yesterday."

I was caught unawares. Like Monica, I had withdrawn from
the group and become a mere spectator.

*She's trying to draw me out, stop me just being a spectator
like her – force me into group participation. She's testing
me too – trying to find out more about me…But I've no
idea how Betty should be treated. Still, I don't really care
what I say, what they think of my answer. I don't think
much of their views anyway – all that silly discussion*

about the lavatory seat. And Monica – I know what she's
up to, even though she may not herself.

Grinning slightly, I replied:

"Well my traumatic experiences with her certainly did provide
me with a few opinions about her – not all of which would bear
repeating! So I'm not sure I'm really all that unbiased!"

Not bad – quite a light-hearted, humorous response. It
should show them I don't care what they think of me, my
views. And it may help counteract the poor impression I
must have made at the beginning of the meeting.

This sense of victory enabled me to tell them quite swiftly and
lucidly all the things I had noticed about Betty: her prediliction
for red; her preoccupation with blood and fire; her morbid song
about her mother whom she declined to draw; the possible
urinary implications of her yellow scribbling. Then all at once I
saw them gazing fixedly at me and was disconcerted.

I'm an acrobat, a solo tight-rope walker at a cabaret,
concentrating on what I'm doing, unaware of the
audience...But suddenly I do notice them. In the
gloaming behind the spotlight their eyes are shining,
piercing through the dimness...now all at once I seem to
be one of them as well as being on the tight-rope. I'm
losing my balance. I must quickly get to the other side,
end the act, before I topple...

I stopped speaking, and in the ensuing silence tried to interpret
their expressions.

They look speculative – but is this a mask? Are they really
condemning?

Gladys stretched her features into a slight smile and said:
"That's very interesting, Hilary."

No it's not. I shouldn't have let myself get so carried away
and air so many views. Now I've given myself away –
offered myself to them irretrievably, with all my
potentialities as a caseworker imprinted indelibly on the
surface. From now on they won't just form vague hypoth-
eses about me; they'll reach concrete, final conclusions.

"Yes, what you have just told us, Hilary, is most interesting,"
Monica for once echoed Gladys. "And while I think of it, I
wonder how you would feel about working with a family where
there are quite a lot of children? Gladys has really got too heavy

a caseload at the moment and would like someone to take over the Kellies."

It's not a request; it's disguised command.

Not waiting for me to answer, she went on, "Gladys and I have been discussing the possibility of your working with this family – haven't we?" (and she glanced at Gladys) "We have talked over how you got on with them this afternoon, and it seems you made a good impression on all of them."

Nonsense – she can't possibly mean it. And after my afternoon with Betty how can she possibly imagine I could cope with a family loaded with children? As I've only just met the Kellies how can she and Gladys have managed to gauge my success with them so soon? She's just praising me to get me to agree to take them over as no one else has time to cope with them. Not that she needs my agreement anyway. And Gladys surely can't have reported all that favourably on my meeting with them?

"I'll try. I'll do my best," I responded.

Chapter 20

Gladys raised her eyebrows so that she looked deceptively supercilious. Speaking very quietly, she said:

"I was just wondering whether anything could possibly be done about one or two little things some of us have recently been feeling just a bit bothered about." She paused, bowed her head and, her speech accelerating to a breathless presto, continued, "It's this business of domestic duties and getting them all properly done and shared out fairly. And of meals, and getting back for them more or less on time and at the same time so as not to make it all too difficult for Mrs Grant." She stopped, blushing slightly.

"Yes, you have raised an important matter – two matters in fact," Monica commented.

"I quite agree," Ben followed. "I'm getting bloody sick of cleaning up all the mess in the General Office every damn morning and evening, then coming downstairs to find the dining-room a shambles – not to mention the state of the bath when I want to take one at night."

"I don't know why you're complaining about that," Nell retorted, "seeing you only seem to have a bath about once a fortnight."

I can't tell from her voice and expression whether she's joking or trying to humiliate him. Perhaps she's punishing him for making her suffer from unrequited love.

No one said anything. Now Ben blushed, then lit a cigarette. The match-strike grated noisily in the brief silence. Monica changed the subject.

"This matter you, Gladys, have raised about punctuality for meals merits, I think, more consideration than we have given it in the past," she said weightily. "For it is, in fact, a question of whether we are ourselves sufficiently altruistic in our general behaviour." She paused, looked round at us all, then, sounding even more ex-cathedra, resumed, "We, as caseworkers, have taken upon ourselves the task of continually and meticulously considering the feelings of other people – of our Clients. But do we invariably give equal consideration to the feelings of those immediately about us? – of Mrs Grant, for example, who takes such pains over cooking our meals, but always against immense odds."

Godfrey rejoined:

"But who takes precedence, Clients or cook? When one's late for a meal it's nearly always because one's been dealing with some family crisis and it would have been disastrous to have left."

"Disastrous is a bit strong," Ben remarked. "Still, I do agree on the whole. A piece of casework with some Client can be ruined if you cut it short. And Mrs Grant knew what she was letting herself in for here when she took the job."

We're more women than men – the men are out-numbered. That may be why they're backing each other up. I'd have expected them to be rivals – though Godfrey doesn't seem to compete with Ben as a lady-killer. He doesn't seem all that interested in us women here. Doesn't he like women? Or has he got very high standards which none of us come up to? He hasn't got a girlfriend somewhere else has he? – I do hope not.

"But Godfrey love, you know meals are not the only things some of us are apt to be late for," Ann remarked.

She's not always punctual herself.

Her gentle sarcasm goaded him into an explosion of self-defence.

"Well I don't myself think mere punctuality for its own sake matters that much," he said loudly, glaring at Ann. "Punctuality for meals, or anything else, is just a formality. There are thousands of much more important things we ought to be discussing – like Mr Dixon's marital problems or what to do about Ronny Parry – something really important to do with the Clients. Why go on and on about if I, or anyone else, happens to be a bit late for Group Discussion? It's so trivial."

He's quite right. I'd like to back him up, but I'd better not.
His outburst is quite refreshing.

Ben bowed his head slightly.

Is he nodding in agreement? Anyway, he's probably acknowledging that they need to present a united male front to us their common female foe. He seems to find girls a perpetual challenge – creatures to be conquered. In a sense, we are his chief enemy.

"Well," Monica stated, "I think perhaps all of us, including you, Godfrey, will surely agree that we want, as far as possible, not to make things too difficult for Mrs Grant. So it is up to all of us to do our best, without seriously impairing our work with our Clients, to be in time for meals and any other regular group activity." She paused.

She's appointed herself group spokesman – but isn't that too authoritative? Isn't she breaking group dynamics rules?

"There will always of course," she went on, "be those exceptional occasions when it is simply impossible to be on time. But I think we should make these occasions as rare as possible, shouldn't we?" Again she paused, staring round at us all.

She's daring us to disagree.

"And now," she said, speaking more briskly, "Reverting to the matter raised by you, Gladys, earlier on – I do so agree that we really must all do our fair share of the domestic work here. This is most important isn't it?" She stopped. There was a vague murmur of assent.

I wonder what she does. Perhaps she's too important to have any domestic tasks.

Glancing at her watch, she continued, "Before we break up

this evening I think we might just run through the list of everyone's duties and consider whether we want to re-allot any."

After this had been done (surprisingly fast), she turned to me and said:

"And then there's just the job of cleaning out the Clients' lavatory before breakfast each morning. I wonder, Hilary, whether you would mind undertaking this task."

Chapter 21

Monica sent for me early the next morning to talk over what I had been doing. I was displeased. By now I had come to accept that no one wanted to discuss my work with me and I no longer particularly wanted them to.

"Well," she said.

She's experimenting again. But I'm not going to respond to that sort of prompting. I won't be pushed into verbal floundering.

I smiled and waited for her to continue. After a short pause she tried again:

"Well, Hilary, now you've been with us for a day or two I wonder what you make of us all?"

What an annoying question. I can hardly say I don't think much of them, and it would sound so fatuous and insincere to say how nice they all are. Anyway, it's what they think of me, not what I think of them, that matters. And aren't we supposed to be discussing my work?

"Well of course," I hedged, "it's early days yet to have formed really definite opinions about anything – really valid ones I mean."

Approving perhaps of this cautious approach (caseworkers not being expected to make snap judgements) she responded with an iota of enthusiasm:

"Yes, I do so agree with you there. It certainly does take time to form really valid opinions. I'm very glad you realise this as it is something all too many social workers – especially beginners – never quite understand. They believe they are endowed with some special gift, intuition, which enables them to fully understand, even empathize with, everyone they meet without

82

ever having to take any time or trouble over doing so."

*She's theorizing – a bit like Godfrey. Did she once upon
a time theorize and generalize as much as he does?
Perhaps she did but found it wasn't useful so stopped,
which may be why she seems to disapprove of him and
his sweeping statements.*

"Casework is a hard and painstaking business. Really getting
to know and fully understand another person and judging what
he is capable of requires tremendous effort, disciplined
application, years of experience and the frustration of often
finding out in the end that you were quite wrong and the Client
could never have achieved what you had hoped."

*For once she sounds sincere. And she's not being vain.
For years she must have striven to make others happy and
again and again been disappointed. She deserves
admiration and sympathy.*

"Yes," I replied thoughtfully, "I suppose years in this work
would be bound to involve immense effort, and often effort in
vain." She glanced swiftly at me then lowered her eyes.

*Does she feel she's exposed herself to a mere Probationer?
Regret, perhaps, her lapse into theorizing?*

"I've read a bit about this intuition some social workers claim
to have," I went on. "But I must say I've never myself found it
easy to sum people up quickly and judge what might be best
for them. I had a friend once who couldn't make up her mind
about something and I used to try and help her – imagine what
I'd do in her shoes –" I stopped short.

*Social workers aren't allowed to put themselves in their
Clients' shoes. This can lead to quite the wrong decision
being made.*

Monica looked sharply at me and I petered out, "But I was
never much help and in the end she went and did something
I'd never have expected."

*I do respect and sympathise with her – all those years of
effort on behalf of others. Perhaps I will reveal a little of
myself, my casework potentialities.*

Regaining self-assurance, I continued, "It would take more
than intuition though, I'm sure, to understand, let alone help,
some of the people I've seen since I came here. Mrs Carter, for
instance, has a list of problems a mile long. They may seem

superficial but I'm sure some run pretty deep." I halted.

She's watching me avidly. I'm playing straight into her hand. I've gone and trapped myself into talking about the Carters, which is bound to lead on to Willy. Can I get off the subject?

"Oh yes, Mrs Carter," she said slowly, then waited for me to go on.

Odd, when I was at the Carters' I wanted to escape and discuss their serious problems with an experienced caseworker, yet now that Monica's waiting to assess my assessment of them I don't want to say anything. Still I must. What did emerge when I visited them?...Plainly their gravest problem – and my main problem as their caseworker – is Willy. But will she understand the dilemma I was in over him? I won't let her know I did nothing about his stealing – she'd be sure to think it cowardly and inefficient. I'll tell her later on when I've managed to do something worthwhile and she's more likely to be lenient and forgive me.

"Even though the family is a closed case," I responded cautiously, "they do still appear to have a number of serious problems –"

I must be careful, as a mere Probationer I shouldn't sound too critical.

"– that is, I mean, although judging from their casepaper everything's greatly improved, they do still seem to have quite a few worries."

"That is most interesting," she replied.

She doesn't mean it.

"I was going to ask you about the Carters. I have already some idea how you got on with Betty and the Kellies, and we have had some discussion about this, so I think – don't you? – it might be wise if now we concentrated on the Carter case."

She's more interested in my attitude to the Clients than in the Clients themselves. And once again she's dehumanizing them – flattening them out between file covers by turning them into a mere "case".

"You say they still have various problems. What in your view is their chief one?"

I'm back at school. Are they just to be useful raw material

*for academic discussion?...I must try and keep off the
tricky subject of Willy's thieving.*

I gave a dull, detailed description of the Walton's cupboard.
*Oh dear, this doesn't sound like a major problem. She'll
think I can't discern serious problems. I must change the
subject, say something that demonstrates a keener
awareness of the family's basic difficulties.*

Hastily I rounded off the Walton's cupboard subject:

"So I promised her I'd tell you about it and ask if someone can
go along and mend it." I paused and swiftly mustered together
in my mind a host of tenuously related matters, then, before
Monica had time to reply, continued, "Because if it fell on any
of the children and they got seriously hurt the family would be
in a fix as Mr Carter's only just back in work after being
unemployed for some time so there are no stamps in his book
to cover medical treatment for them."

I mustn't let on how little I know about the health service.

"Then this, I imagine, would be information very relevant to
the business of Mrs Carter's haemorrhages – assuming she really
is suffering in this way and they aren't actually an emotional
symptom of some deeper conflict –psychosomatic, if you see
what I mean?" Monica did not respond so I continued, "Also of
course to any illnesses the children might get; or accidents, such
as if that wobbly cupboard affair really did sometime go and
crash down on one of their heads or something." I stopped. She
nodded and looked searchingly at me.

*Has she some magnetic power that can draw further
ideas, or anyway words, out of me whether I like it or
not? She's still not satisfied. Better try and forget she's
here – imagine I'm alone with no hypercritical listener
present. Then I may be able to relax and not feel flustered
but concentrate on what we're actually discussing and
say something sensible.*

"For I suppose," I went on, "if he's been out of work for ages
or has had lots of different jobs in a short time this might indicate
that there's some quite serious flaw in his personality – that he's
got psychopathic tendencies perhaps. I gather it's typical of
psychopaths not to be able to hold down any job for long. And
it might also show whether he'd reverted to his earlier ways.
According to the case-paper he used always to be having spells

of unemployment for no very clear reason. Then too, I suppose, it might indicate whether the family now needs more visiting." I paused, then daringly concluded, "Perhaps they were in fact a case that was closed prematurely."

"Yes, I agree with much of what you say," she replied. Perhaps she really did as she did not try to extract further thoughts from me just then. At last sounding interested in the Carters as people, not merely as Probationer-fodder, she continued thoughtfully, "Indeed, if Mr Carter has been out of work for a considerable length of time this will certainly need looking into – though that does not mean of course that the family wouldn't be entitled to free medical treatment. We may have to resume visiting the family regularly again for a while."

Is she suggesting that we form a team of two to rehabilitate the family?

I felt so flattered that I did not listen properly as she continued, even more ruminatively, "I particularly wonder about the children. Joyce, now I come to think of it, said, when we decided to close the case, that she foresaw future difficulties over Kathy – who was then still only a baby. She thought Mrs Carter tended to project too much of her basic frustration on to Kathy. Then there were difficulties over Willy and his relationship with his father. Joyce was afraid he might go off the rails later on." I did not notice the perilous direction she was going in until she said, "I should be very interested to hear how these two are now – especially Willy." I was jolted out of my inattention.

We've got on to Willy. I must at all costs avoid admitting how feeble I was over him. She'd be so contemptuous. Yet I oughtn't to completely block her – she's entitled to some comment on the children. I'll concentrate on Kathy.

"Yes, well, I did see Kathy," I said. "In fact Kathy and her mother in action together. Joyce may not have been far wrong. Mrs Carter certainly did nag. She shouted a bit at her and seemed to consider her a nuisance more than anything. She even called her wicked. I wondered whether I ought to say something to her that might, you know, sort of suggest that saying things like that wasn't exactly very good for Kathy – not saying anything direct I mean, but, well, just sort of dropping a slight hint somehow that she might remember and think over later. But I decided that perhaps, in the circumstances, it might be wiser not to try just then."

*Is she impressed by my caution over advising and
reproving a client?*

"Yes, I expect she would scold Kathy quite frequently," Monica
replied. "One must never forget that there are different social
standards and values."

Isn't that a bit snobbish for a social worker?

"Working class women are apt to nag and shout at their
children, sometimes seeming positively vicious. But this doesn't
necessarily mean they are as angry as they sound. And the
children know this." She paused, then added discouragingly,
"One must always try to look beneath the surface and not be
deceived by the superficial. It will I'm afraid, Hilary, take you
more than one visit to make an accurate evaluation of Mrs
Carter's attitude towards Kathy." To my consternation she now
moved on to Willy. "Willy now," she said, "is the one we all used
to feel most anxious about. Did you happen to see him? – though
of course he should have been at school."

I can't just tell a downright lie to get off the subject.

"Yes, as a matter of fact I did see him for a moment – a split
second," I replied. "He came in while I was there but then went
off again and didn't come back before I left."

"I see. I wonder what sort of boy he's turned into," she said,
actually sounding interested in Willy himself.

"Well you see I hardly saw him, so I can't really tell you much
about him," I half-lied. "He came in just as I was leaving."

Her interest at once shifted off Willy and back on to me. She
regarded me suspiciously.

*She must have noticed my blundering, slight
inconsistency.*

Her look grew steadily keener until it seemed to penetrate my
thoughts. Then, blunting without actually withdrawing her stare,
she remarked surprisingly mildly:

"He used to be such a pale, undernourished looking little boy.
I wonder if he is still so frail and delicate?"

"Yes, he is still thin and pale," I replied, relieved that it was
such a simple question, not requiring any prevarication on my
part. "Mrs Carter said something about his having asthma."

There was an awkward pause as Monica looked hard at me
again.

*She knows quite well I'm holding something back and is
waiting for my confession…I'm in a stifling atmosphere,
emotionally charged, suffocating…This alarming pause
is an empty room; my tension, elastic bands criss-
crossing it, pulled tighter and tighter. They're going to
snap – catastrophe or relief?…It's absurd – here's the
Group Leader staring at me as though she's trying to
hypnotize me. Though now I see this I don't mind any
more. She can't hypnotize me. It's I who can read her
thoughts. I know very well when she's pumping me,
trying to get me to say things I don't want to say. Well
I'm not going to say them…But she actually is a
hypnotist. She's wearing a spangly, clinging, low-cut
tunic. Above it her plumply compressed breasts protrude
indecently. Below are her bulbous thighs. Gladys is
kneeling in front of her, hypnotized, her hands flat
against her thighs…Now the elastic bands have snapped.
I'm laughing inside. I don't care. It doesn't matter what
I say about Willy after all. I don't care what this absurd,
pseudo-hypnotic group leader thinks.*

I broke the silence:

"And I'm sure he's got some behaviour problems – pretty
serious ones." I proceeded to describe quite calmly the pilfering
incident and my subsequent encounter with Willy in his home.
I even explained why I had decided to defer doing anything
about the matter.

Monica listened attentively. When I had finished she nodded
and merely responded:

"Yes I see. What you say certainly does bear out our earlier
concern about his possible development. We shall have to start
working with the family again."

*There isn't a trace of rebuke in her tone. As Group Leader
she may of course like to baffle her subordinates by
capriciously withholding judgement from time to time.
And this may be her way of punishing me for trying to
withhold this vital information about Willy.*

"Well yes, I suppose so. I suppose they will need some more
visiting," I acquiesced.

*What does she think about my procrastination over him?
Should caseworkers ever put off making decisions? But*

I'd better not ask – her answer might be so discouraging and critical.

"So I think – don't you? –" she concluded, "that you should visit them again soon and get a few more precise facts about Willy and the family generally so that we know what line to take with them. And you might also read up about the Health Service and be sure you know how National Insurance works."

She fingered the papers on her desk, and I knew the interview was at an end. I wanted to prolong it, get her to be more precise about the precise facts I was to obtain, but I knew it wouldn't do to stay once I had been dismissed.

"Yes, very well. I'll go and see them again soon," I replied.

"Good; then you will be able to bring back some really useful information," she said with a slight, encouraging smile. I left the room.

Chapter 22

I decided to go straight off to the Carters that morning, but when I returned to the General Office I found the others had different plans for me: Nell wanted me to look after Betty again for a couple of hours; Ann wanted me to take the O'Donnell children to the Head Centre because, she said, it would, apart from anything else, be interesting for me to see how a Head Centre worked. (No one explained what a Head Centre was. I wondered whether it was an I.Q. testing place or a de-lousing clinic.) But I was spared having to choose which of them to disoblige as Gladys cut in:

"Yes but I don't think, love, you'll have time this morning for either Betty or the O'Donnells as Monica's asked you to take over the Kellies. Eva has just been round and sprung a bit of a surprise on me. I forgot to tell you yesterday about Mrs Kelly being pregnant and how difficult it is to get her to go regularly to ante-natal and so on. We didn't think the baby was due for at least another two weeks, but apparently she had to be rushed off to hospital in the middle of the night, and I think – don't you? – that we – I mean you as she's now yours – ought to go and see her in hospital right away and find out how she's getting on and make arrangements with her generally."

Nell sighed and said she supposed Clara would have to look after Betty yet again and Ann decided Godfrey should deal with the O'Donnells. They both left the office.

I looked expectantly at Gladys, hoping she would supply more detailed information. For once she did.

"You see, love," she explained, "we always have difficulty over her when she has babies" (reducing her to the status of a pet dog producing an unwanted litter). "She has no idea how to look after them, and this time it will be even worse. Before, her mother, who's dead now, always used to come and help her cope. At any rate she stopped the babies actually dying of neglect. But now she's dead it's up to us to do all we can to help and advise Mrs Kelly."

Surely not. Am I actually being advised to advise a Client? That's against casework rules. And what an immense task – to be entrusted with the life of a baby. It's a great compliment really, even though it's expecting a bit much of a new recruit.

"So you think I should visit her in hospital this morning?" I asked.

"Yes," she replied. "I definitely do think you should go and see her as soon as possible. She knows and likes you."

What a lie! She's just atoning for her guilt over shifting the huge burden of the family's problems on to me.

"You can find out when she's due to go home and arrange to meet her then and bring clothes from the store-cupboard for the baby. She's in St. Hugh's." She stopped. I was afraid this was all she was going to tell me, however she resumed, "I wonder whether it's another girl. If it's a boy I'm afraid Mr Kelly will take it out of her. He hates boys – or says he does – and he's threatened her with dire consequences if this one isn't a girl."

She sounds concerned about the actual birth of the baby and isn't merely using it as a means of precipitating a Probationer into a suitably problem-ridden household.

"And you can also find out if she's got and done all the necessary things – though I've more or less seen to this already. Still, you might remind her about her Family Allowance application. And you should check whether she's made adequate bedding arrangements for the baby and whether she's got something suitable to bath it in and knows about sterilising the milk bottle and boiling the nappies regularly."

I read up the Kellies' case-paper for about half an hour then set off for St. Hugh's hospital.

I propped my bicycle against the wall of the asphalt yard in front of the main entrance and briefly surveyed the building. Probably it had once been a workhouse. I hoped I never had a baby in such a depressing place. The walls were so encrusted with soot that the hospital appeared to have been built of coal. Chequered with rows of identical windows, it resembled a prison.

As I stood outside the Enquiry Office window I remembered that hospital visiting hours were generally in the afternoon, so perhaps I wouldn't be allowed in. I pressed the bell beside the window. The pane was jerked aside, and there was a dark suited, pale faced man looking out at me – less with his actual eyes than with the highlights of his bifocal lensed spectacles.

"I should like to see Mrs Kelly please. She's in the Maternity Ward," I said, and was told coldly that these were not Visiting Hours so I would have to come back later.

If I return to the Agency with my mission unfulfilled I'll once again be branded as incompetent. I must get him to let me in.

"Yes but I'm a welfare officer from the Hunter Street Problem Family Casework Agency," I explained. "Mrs Kelly is one of our Clients. She's just had a baby and it is exceedingly important for me to see her now."

But he just answered flatly:

"I'm very sorry Madam. I'm afraid it isn't possible to see any patients out of Visiting Hours."

He's infuriating – so impersonal and adamant. And calling me "Madam" when he can see I'm nothing of the sort! He just said it contemptuously because I actually look so young and unimportant. I mustn't show I'm angry though or I'll never get past him.

Dropping my formal tone and sounding almost pleading, I said:

"But this is a quite unusually exceptional case though. Mrs Kelly is one of our very difficult cases – the mother of a Problem Family. She knows next to nothing about looking after babies and needs help and guidance. I should really be most terribly grateful if you would make an exception just this once."

He relented somewhat. Moving his head a degree so that the highlights slid away and I could see his actual eyes regarding me with mild curiosity, he conceded:

"Well, if you'll show me your credentials I'll see what can be done."

Credentials? What does he mean? Are social workers expected to carry cards about with them like journalists to flash in the faces of obstructive officials?

"I'm afraid I haven't got any actual credentials on me," I answered. "But, as I say, I'm from the Hunter Street Problem Family Casework Agency, and it really is extremely important for me to get to see Mrs Kelly just as soon as possible."

Really I suppose it's important for me rather than for her.

But he merely replied:

"I'm very sorry Miss, but I'm afraid I simply can't let you in without some card to show the Ward Sister that you're making a professional visit. It would be against the rules." I gave up and left the hospital.

As I was bicycling away I remembered having noticed a heap of Agency visiting cards on Monica's desk. If Monica were out when I got back I would, I decided, simply go into her office, take one of the cards and promptly return to the hospital. If she were in it would be another matter. I didn't want to confess my foolish lack of forethought, yet it would be unwise to put off visiting Mrs Kelly. If I did Gladys would be displeased and would be sure to tell Monica anyway.

Luckily Monica's office door was wide open and the room empty; but the stack of visiting cards was not on her desk. I was in a quandary: should I risk rummaging about in her desk drawers? What else could I do?

After glancing round the room to see if the cards were somewhere else I opened the desk drawers one by one and, as swiftly and neatly as possible, explored their contents.

My own name typed at the head of an official looking sheet of paper caught my eye and I couldn't resist reading what was on it even though it might be discouragingly uncomplimentary. However, it was merely a string of facts: my age, academic qualification, the names and addresses of those who had written references for me and a note of the Clients I had so far seen. I was relieved (or was I disappointed?) that there were no comments on my performance nor any indication of what future tasks were in store for me.

I had closed the door before starting my search so did not hear footsteps approaching. The door-handle twist gave me a start, and Monica was in the room before I had time to try to look composed. I was still clumsily shoving back the reluctant drawer after cramming in the papers as she said:

"Did you want something Hilary? Are you looking for something?"

Of course I am – why ask? She must be so surprised to catch me like this that even she is nonplussed. But I wish she wouldn't sound so mild. It's far more alarming than if she exclaimed in horror or was terribly indignant. She's just pretending to be calm, deliberately not being angry or reproachful as a punishment – like when we were discussing Willy. Well I'm angry with her now.

Recovering my self-assurance, I re-opened the drawer, methodically straightened the papers, closed it and replied:

"Yes, as a matter of fact I was looking for something – those Agency visiting cards I saw on your desk earlier." Suddenly exhausted by the continuous strain I had been under for the past hour or two, I simply told her what had happened.

Sounding as unruffled as before, she responded:

"Yes, I see. Yes we have got some Agency visiting cards. They're usually kept upstairs in the General Office table drawer. You must help yourself to some."

She would have preferred a confusion of clumsy prevarications to my frank confession – something she could have skilfully penetrated and manipulated. And even now she's not going to reprimand me but leave me uncertain how she really feels.

"Thank you," I replied. "I'll get some when I go up." I paused then dared to add, "I do hope you didn't mind my looking around for them in here? I thought this was where they were kept and there was no one to ask."

"Oh no, that's quite all right," she answered. Sounding slightly indignant she added, "Though it was really rather thoughtless of Gladys not to have warned you about St. Hugh's visiting hours and seen that you had a supply of Agency cards."

*I don't understand: she's blaming Gladys, not me –
sounds genuinely cross with her. So perhaps after all she
wasn't just pretending not to be cross with me. She may
really be a naturally calm person who doesn't like
upbraiding and upsetting others. I'll have to start all over
again trying to work out what sort of person she is.*

"Well yes, but she did give me a lot of useful advice," I replied.
"And I daresay she took for granted I'd know about hospital
visiting hours and so on – as I suppose really I should have."

Sounding all at once rather weary, Monica said:

"Well, we live and learn, Hilary. If I were you I'd go straight
up to the General Office and get some cards, then see if you can
get in your visit to Mrs Kelly before dinner."

Chapter 23

Once the man in the Enquiry Office saw my card he raised no
further objections to my visiting Mrs Kelly. I should turn left
down the main corridor, he said, go up the second long (not
short) flight of stone stairs to the second landing and there turn
right until I reached the lift, beside which were four wooden
steps (easy to miss unless one were on the look out for them),
down which I should descend, then turn right at the bottom.
The Maternity Ward was the third door on the left; just inside
was the small Sister's Office where I should present myself and
my credentials before proceeding to Mrs Kelly's bedside.

He pushed back his window pane, and I set off down the main
corridor, turning right instead of left by mistake.

The corridor was long and dim, with dully gleaming walls
painted some dismal colour. The atmosphere was heavy with
hospital medicinal smell.

I walked some distance without discovering the second long
or short flights of stone stairs. Had I misheard the Enquiry Office
man's instructions? Had he deliberately misdirected me? I halted,
hoping someone would appear whom I could ask the way; but
the corridor remained surprisingly empty.

Should I knock on one of the doors and ask whoever was

inside to guide me on my way, I wondered. I decided not to; for what if I walked in on a doctors' conference or a conclave of Matrons? Presently I reached a door marked "Almoner". A fellow social worker might be sympathetic and helpful, so I knocked on this door.

I entered and found myself in a gleaming office. In the swivel-chair before a shining desk, on which were a dictaphone and a sleek modern typewriter, sat a crisply waved, sharp eyebrowed, bright lip-sticked young woman who looked an intrinsic part of the office equipment.

Oh dear - compared to her I must look so casually dressed and dishevelled. She won't think much of me for losing my way; is sure to be scornful, not sympathetic. I should never have knocked on this door. I only hope the others at Hunter Street don't get to hear about my getting lost. Still, now I'm here I've got to say something.

"I've come from Hunter Street – the Hunter Street Problem Family Casework Agency – to see someone – a woman, a Mrs Kelly – in the Maternity Ward," I floundered. "And I was just wondering if –"

She cut me short:

"Oh yes. You're from the Hunter Street group. Do sit down a minute. I'm sure Miss Homer will be delighted to see you once she's off the 'phone."

I noticed a second door.

So she's not herself the almoner. With any luck Miss Homer will be older and more motherly than this alarmingly immaculate young woman – though someone occupying an inner sanctum guarded by such a sentry may turn out to be a formidably austere official who will treat me with contempt.

The young woman resumed typing. I sat on a chromium and leather chair and waited nervously for the encounter with Miss Homer. I looked round the room.

How amazing that such a hideous, archaic building should contain such a smart, up-to-date office – the office of a social worker moreover. Shouldn't all social workers be too dedicated for such luxury? Am I scornful or envious of her?

Before long a youngish woman stuck her head round the door.

Perhaps she was not really as young as she looked: her cropped, tousled hair gave her the not quite incongruous air of a somewhat elderly undergraduate. In a boyish voice she called:

"Oh Mary, I've contacted Mr Lucas, and he says he'll be round about three. If I'm not back by then get him to wait will you?" Then, seeing me, she came into the room properly. She was dressed in a jumper and corduroy skirt and was wearing lace-up shoes. Her lips were only sketchily tinted. I was relieved; she looked casual, not austere. She smiled at me and Mary stated:

"This is one of the Hunter Street group – sorry, I didn't catch your name. She wants to talk to you about Mrs Kelly."

How confusing. How can I now admit that I've just got lost? And she makes it sound as if there's only one Mrs Kelly in the entire hospital – or anyway as if she knows which one I've come to see. Perhaps Miss Homer knows her all too well – in which case it would be useful to discuss her with her. It would be good to be backed up by someone – though by now of course I've just about got used to the idea of tackling the family on my own. It's a kind of challenge.

"Do come in," Miss Homer said. "I'd be most interested to hear your views on Mrs Kelly – she's one of my fifty dollar problems at the moment."

I followed her into the office. It was cosier and more personal than the outer office. There were two pictures on the walls; one of scarlet, swirling horses; the other of ancient Chinese charging horses. Perhaps Miss Homer's hair was wind-blown rather than tousled (did she even ride a bicycle?) for on the desk was a vase full of wild flowers and on the rug in front of the electric fire a black retriever. The ash-tray on the desk was crammed with cigarette butts and the air tobacco laden – obviously Miss Homer was not an old-fashioned, never-drinking-or-smoking welfare lady.

"So you're one of the Hunter Street group," she said, propping herself on a corner of the desk and vaguely indicating a chair for me. She offered me a cigarette, lit one for herself, inhaled deeply, then went on, "Yes, I'll certainly be delighted to hear anything you can tell me about Mrs Kelly. She really is a problem." She smiled at me and I was immediately tongue-tied.

Whatever can I tell her about Mrs Kelly that would be of

any interest to her?

"Well, you know, I suppose – we think –" I stumbled, "that the main difficulty at the moment – that is, the most urgent one, as of course, as you know, the whole family's weighed down by problems – is this business of the baby. I gather – I've only just taken over the family – that in the past her mother, who's now dead, did most of the looking after of the babies. So this time Mrs Kelly will have to manage on her own. She'll need a lot of help."

Come to think of it, why will she? – most newly-weds manage all right.

Miss Homer looked perplexed.

"I'd no idea she'd just had a baby," she said. "How extraordinary. I'd have thought she'd have told me she was going to. I didn't even realise she was pregnant. Whoever can be looking after it now she's had this accident?"

So we aren't talking about the same Mrs Kelly. What a waste of time and energy it all is. I don't care after all if she does think me silly to have got lost. She's being silly herself.

"I'm afraid we're talking at cross purposes," I said. "The Mrs Kelly I've come to see has just had a baby, not an accident. The man in the Enquiry Office didn't give me very clear directions to the Maternity Ward. I wonder whether you could possibly tell me how to get there?"

"Oh yes, by all means," she replied, sounding a trifle bemused.

She accompanied me into the corridor and directed me concisely on the first stage of my journey, advising me to ask someone else the rest of the route. I went back down the corridor past the Enquiry Office, hoping its occupant did not suddenly slide back the window and catch me retracing my footsteps.

When I reached the first flight of stairs I couldn't remember if it was this or the second flight I was supposed to go up. I decided to try this flight, and ascended, only to find it led to a gentleman's lavatory. Had both the Enquiry Office man and Miss Homer been playing a practical joke on me?

As I paused outside the lavatory the chain was pulled vigorously within then a man emerged. He wore a dark, well tailored suit and had a gold watch-chain across his out-thrust waistcoat. Probably he was someone eminent – a specialist, even a surgeon. Engrossed in his own thoughts, he scarcely seemed to notice me as he passed me on the staircase. Feeling my presence there called for some explanation, I said breathily:

"Excuse me, but I think I'm lost. I'm trying to find the Maternity Ward. I wonder if you could help me please?" He looked at me distantly, and laconically directed me on my way.

I reached the second landing without further difficulty, but, having descended the "easy to miss" short flight of wooden steps, couldn't remember whether to turn left or right. I paused again.

A massive, moustached woman in navy-blue and a frilly, starched cap came clattering down the corridor. She might be an exalted, administrating rather than nursing super-sister, or possibly a matron. As she reached me she glanced at me; then looked at me curiously; then, stopping, stared dubiously at me.

"Are you a visitor?" she reproved rather than asked, then, not waiting for an answer, added sternly, "These are not Visiting Hours. No visitors are allowed in before two."

What about dying patients' relatives? – but I'd better be careful not to annoy such an august personage and risk getting sent away.

Forcing an obsequious note into my voice, I replied:

"No, I see, I'm so sorry," (nearly adding, "Madam"). "But actually I'm not exactly a visitor. I'm a social worker, and I've come to see one of my Clients who's in the Maternity Ward."

"Oh, I see," she said, sounding as though she didn't, or certainly didn't intend to. She inspected me suspiciously for a moment, then continued, "Well you can't go on the ward without credentials. It's a strict Hospital Rule. Anyone wishing to make a professional visit to a patient out of Visiting Hours must have credentials."

She sounded triumphant. Equally triumphant, I replied:

"Yes I know. I'm from the Hunter Street Problem Family Casework Agency and I have a card. I wish to see a Mrs Kelly in the Maternity Ward."

Perhaps she was impressed by my firm tone for, surprisingly, she did not, after all, demand to see my credentials but just said:

"Very well then. In that case I suppose it will be all right – though we don't encourage anyone to visit out of Visiting Hours. The Maternity Ward is the third door on the left." And she clattered on down the corridor.

"Sister's not on today," a slight, young nurse replied when I asked to see the Ward Sister. She sounded peremptory, but did not appear surprised to see me.

"Oh," I responded. "Well I should like to see Mrs Kelly please – Mrs Kelly of 13 Olivia Terrace."

"We've got three Mrs Kellies on the ward just now," the nurse replied. "I don't know their addresses I'm afraid. But that's all right."

Three Mrs Kellies on a single ward! However many can there be in the whole hospital? And why ever did Miss Homer assume it was her particular Mrs Kelly I'd come to see? She must be so engrossed in her Mrs Kelly that she forgot there were any others here. Very praiseworthy in a way. She must be admirably dedicated.

Finding the nurse's final words ambiguous, I pursued:

"Yes, well I'd be ever so grateful if you'd find out for me if I can see my Mrs Kelly for a few minutes please."

"Yes, that's all right," she repeated stiffly. "I'm in charge today." *How surprising – a little thing like her. I can see her striving to hoist some immense, overblown patient on to a commode or shrilly giving orders to all the older, larger, yet junior nurses on the ward…But how can I recognise my Mrs Kelly among all these comatose, nondescript, surprisingly old looking women?*

I approached a patient who, from a distance, looked as though she might be Mrs Kelly.

"Hullo Mrs Kelly," I said brightly.

"Not so good thanks, hen," she replied in an unfamiliar Scottish voice. I had picked one of the other Mrs Kellies.

"I'm so sorry," I said. "I'm afraid I mistook you for someone else." I retreated to the centre of the ward and stood still.

What does she look like? – I can't really remember. And when people are in bed they look different. I hope the nurses don't notice me standing here dithering. And I hope Mrs Kelly doesn't either. It would never do if she realised I can't recognise, remember her.

Having finally decided which face probably belonged to my Client, I found myself at Mrs Kelly's bedside. She seemed neither surprised nor pleased to see me but evidently just took my presence for granted.

"'s boy," she announced gloomily. Forgetting that Mr Kelly had ordered her to produce a girl, I said:

"Oh good. How lovely."

"Lovely indeed!" she exclaimed. Her disgruntled sarcasm reminded me of Mr Kelly's preference. I replied:

"Well yes. Nice, I mean, to have had a baby and everything, and that everything's gone all right." She looked still more disgruntled so I decided to change the subject and asked where the baby was.

"'e's being seen to," she replied. After a short pause she added, "I'll never 'ave no more, that I won't. 'e'll fair kill me."

Who? – husband or baby? Anyway it probably would be best for her to have no more babies.

"Well of course," I remarked, "you could, you know, be steril- ized if you like."

Quite clever and knowledgeable of me to be able to provide this pertinent piece of information.

But sounding even more gloomy, she merely repeated:

"'e'll fair kill me, 'e will."

What can I say? She can't mean Mr Kelly would actually kill her for having produced a boy. Does she mean he'd be furious if she refused to have any more children, got sterilized? He'd be bound to be angry if she tried to stop him having intercourse with her – though it's beyond me why he would want to, with anyone quite so plain and squalid. Do people like him have such insatiable sexual appetites that they'll make do with just about anyone? – what a disgracefully class-conscious notion…Probably he wouldn't want her to be sterilized. He might feel humiliated by having an infertile wife. Then there are so many Catholics in this city, and they're against birth control and sterilization. The Kellies may well be Catholic – Kelly's an Irish sounding name. I may have deeply shocked her by so much as suggesting sterilization. Better change the subject quickly. What would be a safe topic? Let me see, what were all those instructions Gladys gave me? – things I was to find out?

"By the way," I broke the silence, "I hope you've managed to fix up some sort of bed for him?"

A rather confused conversation followed, as Mrs Kelly thought

I meant separate sleeping quarters for Mr Kelly, not a cot for the baby. By the time I had managed laboriously to correct the misunderstanding the dinner trolleys had arrived and nurses were hovering in the vicinity indicating it was time I went.

Walking back down the ward between the two rows of patients I was struck by their uniformity.

Are most people in fact uniform, dull? Perhaps we're all so alike and so dull that no one – or very few – is ever seriously interested in anyone else. However much of yourself you may reveal it rouses very little interest. How depressing... Yet, on second thoughts perhaps it's not so bad, for if no one's really interested in anyone else, then everyone remains separate and undisturbed in their private shells. You never really expose yourself at all.

I cycled back to the Agency feeling all at once free, no longer fettered by anxiety over what the others at Hunter Street thought of me. I felt almost jubilant.

It doesn't matter what I say about myself or how much of myself I may seem to give away to them as, whether they realise it or not, they're really only interested in themselves. They'll never truly know me. I was wrong to think they could take my personality apart and reassemble it.

A gust of wind frisked my hair back off my forehead. I felt buoyant and breezy on the bicycle. No one could seriously manage or damage me.

Chapter 24

During dinner I felt agreeably detached, unaware of a certain tension in the atmosphere and that the others were less talkative than usual. As the meal was drawing to an end Monica said quietly:

"Well then, we'll have our little meeting in my office in about ten minutes' time, shall we?"

The words "little meeting" punctured the trance-like film just then enveloping my mind.

What little meeting? Surely not another group discussion

so soon? But she doesn't seem to be addressing us all, so maybe it's some exclusive little meeting...They aren't going to discuss me are they? I'd like to know what it's all about but I'm sure I'm not supposed to ask.

My carefree mood was not entirely dispelled however and I was prepared to risk being tactless and inquisitive. Back in the General Office I asked:

"What did she mean about a meeting in ten minutes? Is it a continuation of last night's Group Discussion? Are we all supposed to go? What's it all about?"

"Oh it's nothing very much – just that Monica wants to talk over something with one or two of us," Ann replied.

Now I'm sure it's about something significant.

When everyone except Nell had left the room I tried again. If Nell wasn't important enough to attend the meeting it didn't much matter what she thought of me.

"What's it all about? Why's it such a mystery?" I asked.

Glad perhaps to be able to get her own back for being excluded form the meeting, she was prepared to let me in partly on the secret.

"It's about Godfrey," she said in a hushed voice. "Only we aren't actually supposed to know. You'll hear about it later I expect."

I wish she'd tell me more. She's probably asserting her superiority over me by withholding further information.

It was the end of my carefree mood. If Godfrey were being discussed, my turn would surely soon come. I was even more disquieted when Gladys re-entered the room a bit later with the message that Monica wanted to see me. However, I need not have been alarmed. Surrounded by all the others, she was just going out and merely said hurriedly:

"Oh Hilary, I suggest you do your phoning this afternoon while we're all out and you have the place to yourself."

"Phoning?" I queried.

"Yes phoning," she repeated, sounding a trifle impatient. "You'll need to do some about the families you've been visiting won't you?" She paused, looked hard at me, then went on, "There will be Mrs Carter's doctor, won't there? And shouldn't you contact the Probation Department about Willy? – though of course you'll need to be very careful and tactful about how you do this. Then don't you think you should get in touch with the

Assistance Board about Mr Carter? – but use your discretion. Only contact those you feel you really must."

I went back upstairs feeling bewildered. Nell had gone. It was the first time I had been alone in the General Office. Almost immediately the telephone rang. I was used to one of the others answering it and let it go on ringing for a few seconds before I realised it was up to me to answer.

Oh dear – supposing I don't take in what is said? Some client may be in the throes of a crisis. And if it's a city official I'll be nervous and say something silly or muddled and let the Agency down.

"Hullo," I said into the receiver. A blurred male voice steeped in the local accent uttered an incomprehensible jumble of syllables, then stopped.

He must be a Client. I'll have to ask him to repeat it all. Can't be helped if he's annoyed or thinks me stupid.

After a brief pause, enunciating very carefully and slightly raising my voice, I said:

"I wonder, would you mind repeating that? – saying it again please?"

The incoherent jumble of words was obligingly repeated – or presumably it was, although he might have said something different this time. I managed to distinguish what I thought might be the word "Nell".

But perhaps that's wishful thinking. Still, it gives me a pretext for handing him over to Nell and sparing myself further embarrassment.

Before the spate of incoherence had quite subsided I interrupted:

"Oh, you want to speak to Nell do you? Just hang on a moment please." I promptly put down the receiver without waiting for a reply and went off to look for her.

I searched the building in vain. Everyone had gone out, including even Clara. I returned unwillingly to the General Office, picked up the receiver and said:

"Are you still there?" – hoping with all my might he wasn't. He was.

By now I had calmed down somewhat and was better able to concentrate on what he said. This time I managed, or thought I did, to pick out one or two with any luck key words and phrases, including "our Stella", "baby", "St. 'ugh's 'ospital", "'ome Thursday or Friday", "dole Tuesday", "needs overcoat an' shoes" and "I'm going to see Joe in Buckingham Christmas".

The telephoner seemed prepared to continue his monologue indefinitely. Then all at once he took me by surprise, halting abruptly on a questioning note, saying, as far as I could make out:

"The Missis says can you?"

What on earth does "the Missis" want me to do?

While listening hard to him I had, at the same time, been busy trying to fill in the gaps between the odd words and phrases I thought I heard in an effort to concoct them into some sort of logical story. For it was important that I passed on a reasonably lucid message to Nell or whoever was in charge of this Client. It didn't occur to me that I myself might be required to give an instant answer, advice or opinion, so I was caught unawares by the question.

Let me see now, what does he seem to have said so far? Probably he's got a wife called Stella who, like Mrs Kelly, has just had a baby in St. Hugh's – did I even see her this morning? – who's due out of hospital on Thursday or Friday and possibly needs an overcoat and shoes to go home in which her husband, being on the dole, can't afford and which she therefore hopes we'll supply. But the bit about visiting Joe in Buckingham at Christmas is puzzling. Perhaps that was part of a subsequent story. But if so then his concluding question too must have applied to the subsequent story and wasn't after all about his wife, baby or clothes. And why would anyone on N.A.B. be going miles away to Buckingham to visit a friend? Have I misheard everything? It would be wisest to make some vague, non-committal response to what he may have been saying.

"Home Thursday or Friday you say," I remarked.

Repeating what he appears to have said seems safe, and it's a way of gaining time in which to decide what to say next.

Hoping to satisfy him and end the telephone call by offering something a little more positive, I added,

"I'll let Nell know as soon as I see her. And I do hope all goes well. You'll let us know immediately if anything crops up, won't you?"

I should not have ended with a question. It prompted a further unintelligible spate of words. Presently he again ended by asking:

"Can you?"

He sounded more urgent this time. Clearly he was not to be fobbed off with vague kindly comments and offers of unspecified help. I felt obliged to say:

"I wonder whether you'd terribly mind just saying that again? – this line's dreadful. I'm so sorry, I didn't just quite catch absolutely everything you were saying."

There followed a further more or less incoherent stream of words. By now he sounded peevish, but this time he ended quite distinctly by asking:

"Can you 'elp me out with an overcoat an' pair o' shoes for me job?"

So he wants a coat and shoes for himself, not for his wife
– like that Charly Dale. I must have got the bit about his
being out of work right – like Charly Dale again, needing
new clothes to start a new job.

"Yes, I'm sure we can fix you up," I replied. "We've got quite a lot of second-hand clothes here I think – though you'd better ask Nell about this as she's your worker isn't she?"

I suggested that he come round to the Agency that evening; then, deciding I had done all I could for him, cut into his prolonged but this time fairly satisfied sounding reply:

"Well then I'll tell Nell, and we'll expect to see you round here about seven. So goodbye for the moment." I quickly replaced the receiver.

Chapter 25

Next I had to make telephone calls about my own Clients. I sat down at the table to think out what to say.

Why has Monica told me to contact officials to learn more
about my Clients? Surely this is breaking a cardinal
casework rule? – you're never supposed to seek or give
information about your Clients without first getting their

permission. Are our sort of Clients such extreme cases that we're allowed to break, bend, the rules a bit on their behalf?...I expect anyway Monica enjoys discussing Clients behind their backs with other social workers and officials...I'll begin with Mrs Carter's doctor. This should be a fairly short, easy telephone call to make and will break me in gently. But first I'd better read up about how the Health Service works.

I glanced around in vain for some book or pamphlet on the National Health Service, then dialled Dr Smale's number.

He sounds genial and elderly – as though he might be bald, bland and stout.

He would be only too pleased, he assured me, to try to answer any questions I cared to ask about any member of the Carter family. He was, he said, only too concerned about them and ready to cooperate in any way he could that was likely to promote their welfare. I put the receiver down.

That's reassuring.

I made notes about the conversation.

Though now I come to think of it I haven't actually learned anything more about the family's health. Perhaps, despite his apparent concern, he doesn't really know the family very well but didn't like to admit it. I still don't know why Mrs Carter has haemorrhages and if they're serious, or if Willy's still got asthma, or whether ill-health has been the main cause of Mr Carter's unemployment. Yet I talked to Dr Smale for at least ten minutes. Did I, in trying to overcome my shyness and impress him, do too much of the talking myself?...I'll tackle the Assistance Board next and leave the Probation Department and the tricky business of Willy's delinquency till last...but why am I supposed to be ringing the N.A.B.? to ask about the overlay they gave the Carters? But there doesn't seem to be any problem about that...I suppose Monica meant me to ask them about Mr Carter's employment pattern.

To my dismay the telephone directory contained a long list of local N.A.B. offices situated in every district of the city. I had no idea which one was nearest to the Carters', and when I studied the map found that Danbey Buildings was about equi-distant from the offices in two adjacent districts. One was possibly a fraction closer to Danbey Buildings than the other so I decided to dial its number.

A robot-like female voice immediately announced:

"Newcombe Grove Assistance Board Area Office can I help you?"

"I was ringing about a family called Carter," I began, but the voice cut in:

"Their address please." When I had answered the voice responded, "Just a moment please."

I waited several minutes before the voice returned, only to ask:

"What address did you say?" I was annoyed. After again stating where the Carters lived I again waited. Presently another voice, male this time and sounding less clockwork, enquired:

"Are you still there?" I assented and he continued, "You did say the Carters of Danbey Buildings?" The question must have been rhetorical for he promptly added, "I'm afraid there's no one of that name with that address on our files. It's outside our area. I suggest you try the Glanville Street office, which is in the adjoining area."

I looked up the Glanville Street Office number all over again, rang it and waited an unduly long time. I was so impatient by the time a meek, middle-aged woman's voice said:

"Hullo, Glanville Street. Is there anything I can do for you?" that I replied quite brusquely:

"Yes there is. I'm speaking from the Hunter Street Problem Family Casework Agency. I want some information about a family I'm in touch with – the Carters of 15c Danbey Buildings."

"Oh, the Danbey Building Carters," she replied, a just off-jolly note in her voice.

Are they the enfants terrible of her office?

"Just a moment please. You'll need to talk to Mr Curtis about them."

Mr Curtis sounded bluff and hectoring. Unprompted, he launched into a semi-tirade semi-lament about the number of times in the past year one or other of the Carters had arrived at his office penniless and pleading for assistance because Mr Carter, for no good reason, was out of work yet again. He was, he said, only too glad to hear someone was at last taking the family in hand again, as they had been in all sorts of trouble, ranging from court appearances for breaking into their gas meter and pawning all their bedclothes to being blackmailed by local money-lenders. He sounded, nevertheless, genuinely concerned about the Carters. Perhaps his blunt tone concealed a kindly nature. He certainly had no qualms about breaking the "Confidence-of-the-Client" rule – which he may never have heard of anyway.

By the end of this conversation I felt decidedly more cheerful.

Surely I've at last managed to glean some useful information about the family? Monica should be impressed.

I hastily noted down the gist of the conversation before I forgot the details. I was about to ring up the Probation Department when Nell entered the room. She sat down in silence at the opposite side of the table and started to thumb through a casepaper. I was displeased; I didn't want an audience when I made my telephone call.

"One of your Clients rang up an hour or so ago," I said. "I took the call as there was no one else here. I hope that was all right?" Still thumbing through the casepaper, she replied:

"Oh yes. Who was it?" She sounded bored. I realised that, absurdly, I had failed to get the man's name.

"Oh God, how crazy of me – I went and forgot to ask who he was," I answered, blushing, and quickly added, "It was the first time, you see, I'd ever actually answered the phone here, and he – it was a man – was extremely difficult to understand."

Nell did not seem vexed. Her lack of concern was even a trifle aggravating. She just said:

"Oh," then, as an afterthought, "Yes, well what was the message?"

"Well, as I say, he was practically incomprehensible," I repeated. "It was as if his speech was sort of all dialect and no language, if you see what I mean." I paused and looked hopefully at her, then went on, "But as far as I could make out his wife's just had a baby in St. Hugh's Hospital, and is, I think, due out on Thursday or Friday. Then he said – or I think he did – something about starting a new job and wanting us to give him a new overcoat and shoes."

Nell still did not look up.

Is she shy? Does she always find it hard to look directly

at people until she knows them well? Poor thing.

Then after a minute raising her head and frowning slightly, she said:

"That's strange. I haven't got any Clients like that. Are you sure he was my Client? – it all sounds a bit like the Kellies. She's gone into St. Hugh's to have a baby. Are you sure he wasn't Mr Kelly?"

"He couldn't possibly have been, I don't think," I replied.

How preposterous if all along it had been one of my own Clients on the phone.

"He said he was yours – at least I think he did – I'm sure he did."

Could I have possibly been mistaken?

"Anyway, I did look all over the house for you, but I couldn't find you anywhere."

"Yes, well I've been out, visiting the Higsons," she replied, sounding for some reason defensive. She returned to her casepaper. After a moment or two I resumed:

"He did – at least I'm pretty sure he did – though it was so very hard to understand him properly – say something about going to Buckingham, or somewhere, for Christmas, to see someone called Joe or something."

This solved the problem. At last looking directly at me, Nell said:

"Oh, it must have been Charly Dale. He's got a son called Joe at an approved school in Birmingham. He usually goes to see him at Christmas. And he's got a speech defect. He's Ben's though, not mine."

"Oh well, I don't know, but I'm sure – I could swear – he mentioned your name, so naturally I took him to be one of yours," I replied.

All clear at last. But what a job it's been trying to get everything straightened out. And I was actually talking to Charly Dale himself. I almost feel I know him, yet even though the man on the phone reminded me of him I didn't realise it was Charly Dale. Somehow I'd imagined he'd be a youth – just starting on a new job – not a family man. And anyway someone surely said he was to have got his clothes and started work yesterday?

"I know what must have happened," Nell explained. "His sister-in-law, Mrs Green, who's always round at their house, is

109

called Bell. I expect actually he was talking about her."

So in that case the "Stella" I thought I heard him mention was probably Bell too...I must end this tiresome conversation.

"Oh dear," I said, "I'm really most awfully sorry. Anyhow, I suggested he should come round this evening about the clothes." To prove I had been sensible over at least one thing I quickly added, "I didn't think I ought to make any really definite promise about giving him clothes or anything in case it wasn't the best policy in his case – I mean I decided it would be best if his own caseworker decided about that, if you see what I mean."

"Yes," she replied. She paused, then went on, "I'll tell Ben – I don't think he meant to go out this evening. He'll be very glad to hear about the baby. They were so wanting another."

Could I have actually got the entire message wrong? His wife may not have had a baby at all.

Nell rose from the table. A moment or two later the tea-bell rang. I was relieved; I could put off ringing up the Probation Department.

Chapter 26

When tea was over Godfrey said:

"Come on then, Hilary. Let's get ready. We're going out this evening aren't we?"

I was delighted although taken aback. He had said nothing about taking me out that evening. He had hardly spoken to me all day.

As we were walking along (he didn't say where) he asked what I was doing at the weekend. I wondered if he were going to invite me to spend it with him, but disappointingly he merely advised me to spend it away from the Agency.

"It's vital you know," he said, "to get away for weekends – especially at first." He abruptly changed the subject, "Have you any interests Hilary?"

"Interests?" I echoed, fumbling to switch my thoughts on to a new topic.

"Yes, interests," he repeated. "It's vitally important to have interests – and so few social workers do seem to have any."

How sweeping. I must get him to be more precise.

"You mean hobbies?" I responded. "Like playing the piano, bird-watching or something?"

"Yes, well hobbies if you like – anything like that, or general interests."

Where are we going? What are we going to do? We're just wandering down Hunter Street.

"Yes, there is a particular thing I rather like doing," I answered. "Not that I'm much good at it." I stopped. I was reticent about my occasional urge to compose music in case people were disbelieving or thought me conceited. But I had roused his curiosity.

"What is it? Do tell me," he asked.

"Well actually," I said, "I sometimes try to compose a bit – compose music."

With any luck such an unusual, aesthetic hobby will impress him.

"Nothing much of course. Not whole symphonies or concertos. Just pieces for two or three instruments."

"My word, you must be very talented!" he exclaimed. "I'm tone-deaf. Can't sing a note in tune. All my family try to avoid sitting next to me in Church."

How disappointing. It would have been nice if we'd both enjoyed music. And why sound so proud of being tone deaf? Astonishing that he ever goes to Church. I'd have thought he'd have been an atheist. Perhaps he only goes when he's at home just to please his family – only I wouldn't have thought he'd have compromised his principles for anyone – that he'd even be unselfish enough to...Anyway, he's a fine person and I love him. I'll think about something else – the scene around us.

The city's very ugliness made it curiously beautiful just then. Down steep, thin streets; between massive, soot-encrusted buildings, I caught tantalising glimpses of the spread-out city, delicately filigreed away into the distance, diaphanous in the evening light. The sky looked somewhat stormy, full of voluminous or tattered clouds, apricot, grey and mauve, separated here and there by triangles of pure turquoise and criss-crossed with pencil lines of tram and trolley wires. The sky was

111

faintly reflected on the cobbles below, transforming them into a choppy, sunset sea. Further on the smooth tarmac, still wet after a recent shower, was bewitched with a sheen of pale mauve and orange and intricately geometried with tram lines at the road junctions.

He must have just meant to be funny. I'll copy his mood.

"Oh dear," I said, "I'll make a point of keeping well away from you then if we ever happen to be in Church together!"

I don't want my musical hobby to create too much of a gap between us.

"Not that I'm actually much of a singer myself though," I added. "I never made the college choir."

Dismissing music he went on:

"As far as I'm concerned it's politics, world affairs, that are my main interest."

"Oh yes," I responded, "You're worried about the ineffectiveness of UNO."

As before, he needed only the slightest impetus to launch into a lengthy discourse on the subject.

"So I'm sure you'll agree," he stated as, somewhat later, he halted abstractedly at the entrance to a dreary looking pub, "that the only real answer is the establishment of another world organization with real power." He opened the pub door, began to enter, then, remembering his manners, stood aside to let me in first.

The bar was crowded with working class people of all races. Most were probably regular customers as they looked at us rather curiously as we entered. Godfrey appeared oblivious of them. He pushed his way through the crowd up to the beer puddled bar. He didn't offer to find me a seat so I followed in his wake.

Propped up against the bar, his elbow carelessly planted in a beer puddle, his chin cupped in his hand, he looked at me with glazed, unseeing eyes, so absorbed in his own train of thought that he was probably barely aware of my existence.

"I'm very interested in a plan for a new world movement," he continued. "A scheme for holding world-wide elections and having a world police force. I went to a big meeting about this in London not long ago and I'm seriously thinking of getting in touch with the organization and getting involved." He paused, and I asked a few appropriate questions.

112

I'm sick of this subject. Can't we talk about something else now? I'd like to hear his views about the Agency. There are so many questions I'd like to ask him about the work – about the Health Service and National Insurance, other city welfare organizations, Monica's policy, what he thinks of the others. He's the only one I dare ask such questions.

But he continued to hold forth about the new world movement, and I began to feel critical.

If he went to this big meeting in London some time ago, why's he done no more than make enquiries about how to join the movement?

I began to get restless.

Are we going to spend all evening in this pub? And he didn't even bother to ask whether I like drinking. He just seems to take for granted we like doing the same things – a compliment in a way I suppose.

At last the bartender got round to asking what we wanted.

"Pint of bitter," Godfrey promptly answered, adding, "What'll it be Hilary?"

It would be safest to ask for beer too – though it's not really a girl's drink. Anyway I loathe it. And I don't want to copy him – just be his friendly shadow – even though I would like to be at one with him. Still, I don't want to be blotted out. I'll ask for something quite different, a bit unusual. That'll remind him I'm an individual.

"I'll have a calvados please," I replied. He laughed.

"Try again, Hilary," he responded. "This isn't France or the West End you know. They don't run to anything so classy in this neighbourhood."

The bartender's initial expression of slightly belligerent surprise swiftly turned into amusement too, then expanded into a guffaw.

"No Miss, this ain't no Ritz nor Riviera!" he echoed.

I feel daft. I should have realised it was a preposterous request.

"Well," I rejoined, "we were in the middle of such a highbrow cosmopolitan discussion that I thought I'd better match it with a high fallutin foreign drink. Still, a gin and lime will do."

We sipped our drinks in silence for a few minutes, then I said:

"Going back to music, are you at all keen on it yourself? – I mean do you ever go to concerts or operas?"

Perhaps it will emerge that we do have a mutual cultural interest. He might even invite me to go to an opera or concert with him – or even to the ballet or a foreign film. What about a film this evening? – it's still not too late.

"Oh yes," he replied. "I go to all the concerts and recitals I can get to. And I specially like oratorios – particularly when performed in cathedrals."

How surprising.

"I enjoy symphonies and so on too, but they're so cold and impersonal compared with vocal music aren't they? There's so much humanity in the sound of the human voice. Although I can't sing a note myself I did play the harp for a while a year or two ago."

Astonishing – someone so often lost in cool abstract thought liking singing because it's warm and personal. And how incredible that he took up the harp, considering he's tone-deaf.

"How amazing!" I exclaimed. "I mean the harp's one of the most difficult instruments to play. Have you got one of your own?"

"Oh no," he replied. "It was just that an aunt left my mother one in her will and it seemed a pity to waste it." He did not enlarge on the subject.

"I can play the piano, and the violin a bit," I said humbly.

"Yes. I used to play the piano too when I was at school. My mother made me," he responded. "But music's not really the most important thing is it? It's only interpretive, and it's so divorced from reality. Painting and writing now – they're a different matter. I was quite keen on sketching at one time and tried my hand at a few portraits. But now I'm concentrating on a scheme for a novel – a novel about the dilemma of modern man trying to find himself."

If only he wouldn't generalize about music. And he's really quite a dilettante, taking up one thing after another enthusiastically then casually dropping them. Is he the same about people? Has he had a succession of girl-friends, dropping each in turn when he got tired of her?

For a while we discussed what he had just said. He ordered more drink and we both became mellowed – he more considerate and attentive to what I was saying; I no longer slightly irritated by him. I decided to change the subject: ask him practical questions about the work. He did not give me precise answers but he sounded so amiable that I, having by then had three gin and limes, was deceived into believing he had. Suddenly I felt rash.

"Look Godfrey," I said, "Tell me, will you – you must have some idea. How am I making out here? What are they all saying about me? Do they – do you – think I'll add up?"

The directness of my question sharpened me up and I was aggravated by his ambiguous reply:

"Add up I don't think it's a question of adding up or not adding up. It's what one makes of oneself in a situation that counts, isn't it?"

He's as bad as Gladys. Is he deliberately evading the question? – He may of course be a bit drunk and vague and rambly by now I suppose.

"Yes, but never mind about that," I persisted. "I'd just very much like to know what the general opinion about me is by now."

Braced up by my impatient tone perhaps, he replied directly:

"Oh, we all like you very much, Hilary." He looked at me with great concern. None the wiser, I tried once more:

"Yes, but I don't mean that – about whether people like me as a person. What I want to know is what they think of me by now as a caseworker." I paused, then, dreading his possible reply, added, "But I daresay you don't know. They may not have talked about his publicly."

"Well you know what they are," he hedged. "Pretty queer lot really, aren't they? I don't myself set much store by their opinions anyway – not that one usually finds out what they think till too late."

Has he been harshly treated himself? He sounds very bitter.

"I mean, take Monica for example," he went on. "A fat, pompous, middle-aged spinster, preaching but never practising – except when she practises on us, her subordinates, getting us into absurd, degrading situations. She thrives on sycophancy. Then Gladys, a sycophant if ever there was one – a real sucker, with so little in her life she has to survive on gossip and her

Clients' problems and devotion. As for Ben – a clown with only one thought in his head. And Ann's as two-faced as they come. Nell's the only one with the slightest grain of integrity."

Such disgust can mean only one thing – they must have decided at the "little meeting" to sack him....Some of his opinions about the others are surprising. Fancy Nell being his favourite. And I wouldn't have thought Ann was two-faced – she seems the friendliest, most open of them. But appearances can be deceptive. I must be more on my guard.

"It's too soon of course for me to have formed definite views about people here yet," I responded. After a brief silence he stated:

"I'm leaving you know." I nodded. "It's the way they go about things," he went on. "One minute it's all: 'Godfrey love, do this and that would you? Mend the Owens' window love,' and so on. Next moment you're sacked."

Whatever can I say? It would be tactless to ask a lot of questions. He seems almost pathetic now, all his belligerence faded. It's quite embarrassing.

"How do you know for certain?" I asked.

"Oh I know all right. Of course I know," he replied. "Come on, let's get out of here." He put down his still half-full glass, then, not waiting for me to answer, turned and pushed his way through the jostling crowd to the door.

Our evening was over. We were on our way back to Hunter Street. Godfrey was in no mood for any further entertainment. I had to hurry to keep up with him as he strode along in silence.

The evening had been so disappointing that I tried to think of something else. I noticed that the orange street-lamp beams, straining down through the fog-hazed night, were tent-shaped, and for a moment I felt I was under cover, sheltered by these cosy triangles of light from the threatening black above. But then I realised that tents, shelter, cosiness were all an illusion – like the illusion I had been having about Godfrey and myself. It had been pure fantasy to believe that, as fellow-Probationers, we had been snugly sheltering together in mutual suffering and commiseration from our threatening senior colleagues. There was, I could now see, no real bond of common interests uniting us. Our approaches to life were quite different. And as he was leaving the Agency I would no longer be able to derive even an illusory sense of security from his presence.

Chapter 27

I took Godfrey's advice and went away to visit some friends in a nearby town at the weekend.

Early on Monday morning Monica sent for me. Anticipating another lengthy interview, I was relieved when it turned out that the summons was merely to remind me to write up accounts of my interviews with my Clients and my telephone calls about them in their casepapers.

"I did jot down a few notes as soon as I'd made the phone calls," I said proudly.

"Good," she replied. "Also it might be wise if you contacted Mrs Kelly's Health Visitor. You'll have to find out who she is – that is, you might consider whether it would be a good idea to do this. Then you can check up on her arrangements for visiting Mrs Kelly and plan your own visiting schedule accordingly."

I assented and returned to the General Office, not quite sure why I was to ring up the Health Visitor.

Shall I put off telephoning till the others, or anyway most of them, have left the office?

Suddenly feeling unaccountably blasé, I just asked:

"Anyone going to use the phone or is it O.K. if I do?"

The telephone call went quite well. The others all seemed too busy to be a hypercritical audience. I caught the Health Visitor just before she set off on her rounds. She had a young, friendly voice. Reassured, I felt relaxed and now half wished the others would listen.

The Health Visitor simply took for granted I wanted to know everything she could tell me about Mrs Kelly's health and the family generally. I took in all she said and asked one or two pertinent questions which I hoped the others overheard. The conversation went so well that I decided, as a reward, to defer ringing up the Probation Department about Willy Carter. Instead I would write up reports of all my interviews and telephone calls.

This proved harder than I had expected. Agency reports were

117

not written as consecutive narratives but broken down under separate headings such as: "Husband", "Wife", "Children", "Health", "Cleanliness", "Employment", "Special Problems". It was hard to decide which item out of the confused information I had by then obtained should go under which heading. Should Mrs Carter's haemorrhages go under "Wife", "Health" or "Special Problems"? And what should I put down for the Kellies' "Bedding Situation"? I had not gone upstairs. Very likely they had no beds.

One by one the others left the office, till only Ann remained. She appeared engrossed in a massive file, so this, I decided, would be a good moment to telephone the Probation Department. I tried to but their line was out of order.

I returned to my reports. Now the others had gone I was no longer tempted to stop working and listen to tantalising scraps of conversation, so I soon finished my writing.

What next? There's no point in going to the Kellies' and I'd better not visit the Carters again till I've contacted the Probation – though on second thoughts I may as well go and see them. I've got to do something and no one can say I haven't tried to ring the Probation Department. I'll just have to do the best I can if anything really tricky crops up. But first I'll glance through their casepaper again.

This took longer than I expected; the file was too bulky and detailed to skim through. Often it was barely legible. The more I read the more perplexed I became. What line should I take with Willy?

Presently I stopped reading and stared abstractedly at Ann seated opposite.

Could she help me? She seems wise and experienced and also sympathetic and a good listener. I'll forget what Godfrey said about her.

"Are you terribly busy Ann?" I asked. She looked up from her file and replied:

"I've got to get this thing read and summarized, but I can spare you a few minutes." She smiled encouragingly.

"It's just that I'm a bit sort of bogged down just now about this Client of mine, Willy Carter," I said.

"Oh yes, Willy Carter," she responded pensively. "I've often wondered how he was getting on these days. Joyce always felt he was the family's number one problem."

She was evidently inviting me to continue so I told her about his recent behaviour.

"So what do you think should be done?" I concluded. "I've had so little experience that I feel a bit at a loss about what to do or not do next."

"Why 'not do'?" she promptly responded.

How do I answer that?

Slowly I responded:

"Well, I suppose I mean that it might be, so to speak, so easy to, well, go and completely put one's foot in it in such a situation – if you see what I mean? I mean, one must try and be aware of all the possible snags and pitfalls, mustn't one, and tread very warily?"

"I don't agree at all," she rejoined quite vehemently. "It's no use being over-cautious. You'll never get anywhere that way. You must remember you can't really harm your Clients, not seriously. Most of them are too near rock-bottom anyway – our sort of Clients that is. Whatever blunders you make will harm you much more than them – hinder you, I mean, from making a useful relationship with them and so making any progress."

How amazing! All the casework textbooks I've read have advised social workers to handle their Clients as carefully as Dresden china – never to say the wrong thing at the wrong moment or use the wrong tone.

"Oh, I'd never looked at it that way," I replied.

I don't really want to change my approach. She's making casework seem much easier and clumsier than I'd supposed it was. She seems to be saying caseworkers don't after all have the power to affect their clients' lives, destinies, even indirectly. That's a relief in a way; still, I'd like to think the job did require great skill and insight.

Sounding a shade resentful, I broke the brief silence:

"Yes, well, but what about the Carters? Can you possibly advise me how to tackle Willy?"

I suppose, though, one should never "tackle" a Client. And I'm asking her to break a cardinal rule – if advising clients is forbidden then presumably advising colleagues how to deal with them is forbidden too. Still, perhaps it doesn't matter. She seems so unorthodox she probably won't mind breaking rules and answering my question.

Perversely she did seem to mind.

"No, I can't very well do that," she answered. Sounding rather like Monica, she continued, "No caseworker can or should advise another about what action to take over a particular Client. You see they don't as a rule actually know the Client personally – or not very well. You could have discussed the family with Joyce of course if she were still here, as she used to work with them. As it is the best thing to do would be to read their casepaper carefully and thoroughly." She paused and studied me.

"Yes, I've been trying to do that," I mumbled.

"Well then," she continued, "you might try following this up by having a sort of dialogue with yourself. Ask yourself all sorts of questions like: Why might Willy need to steal? Is it because the family's poor and needs more food? Is it because he's bored, or because he feels unwanted and steals as a substitute for love? Is he copying his father by being a criminal? Try doing this and you may find you can reach some sort of answer. It may turn out to be the wrong one of course, in which case you'll have to start all over again. But no one else can really tell you what to decide." She stopped for a second, then resumed, "Take my Mrs Owens for example."

I don't want to hear about her Mrs Owens. Why can't she stick to the Carters?

"I've managed to develop the sort of relationship with her which would make it impossible for anyone else to act just as I am in the situation. I suppose she's got a real Freudian transference on me. It's rather wonderful in a way."

She sounds almost dreamy. She must like Mrs Owens having a Freudian transference on her. Is she a bit like Gladys in fact – needing people to need her, be dependent on her? Could this be why she so deplored this trait in Gladys the other evening?

Speaking more briskly, Ann concluded, "So if I were you I'd try asking myself some of these questions and see where they lead even if you do go wrong and have to keep trying all over again."

"Thank you very much. That's very helpful," I replied. "I'll certainly give it a try. I was quite at sea before – hardly seemed to know how to even start thinking about it all."

"That's all right. You'll be all right, Hilary," she said.

Encouraged by her slightly quizzical smile, I decided to be daring. I asked outright:

"How do you think I'm getting on? Am I doing things the right way? It's useful – isn't it? – to hear what other people think about how one's doing otherwise one can't ever learn."

Her smile faded and she looked at me thoughtfully.

Can she tell how anxious I am? I wish she'd say something. This silence is embarrassing.

After a few moments she replied:

"It isn't easy to venture an opinion about your – or any worker here's – progress. For one thing you hardly ever see other caseworkers in action, so you can only judge by results. And you've only been here a short time. I can't answer that sort of question. You must ask Monica." She stopped. I must have looked a trifle desperate for she resumed, "As I think I told you the other evening, I felt terribly tired and depressed when I first started here. It's natural to begin with. I expect you're feeling a bit like this at the moment. But you'll soon find your feet, I'm sure." She paused, then went on, "I found your comments on Betty at the Group Discussion quite interesting. I didn't agree with them all – but they showed you have good powers of observation. And you heard what Gladys said about how you got on with the Kellies; and now the family's been handed over to you. So I wouldn't be too worried, Hilary. There's the credit as well as the debit side." She gave me a broad smile then returned to her reading.

I was frustrated by her ambiguity. I tried to concentrate on the Carters' file but my thoughts kept wandering.

Does she or doesn't she think I'm progressing satisfactorily, and, if not, what's wrong with my approach?

Eventually I gave up trying to read and set off for the Carters'.

Chapter 28

"Oh it's you," Mrs Carter said as she opened the door.

Is she pleased to see me or merely indifferent?

She led me straight down the passage to the living-room. Pausing on the threshold, she announced with a grin, "You're too late!"

Whatever for? Willy? Has disaster befallen him – police already brought him to court? Is he already imprisoned in some remote approved school? But why's she smiling?

Her grin broadened. She looked positively gleeful.

There can't have been a disaster. What a relief.

"Yes, you're too late," she repeated.

Perhaps she can tell I'm bewildered and is deliberately prolonging my suspense. Harrassing caseworkers may give her a pleasant sense of power.

After a short pause she stated:

"'s been fixed."

I must have still looked perplexed – but as caseworkers were supposed to be problem-solvers who knew everything she sounded faintly contemptuous as she continued, "Cupboard's fixed. You're too late. 'e done it 'imself."

Oh, she's talking about that Walton's cupboard. But it's all a bit baffling. She said before she didn't need our help because Walton himself could fix it, yet now she seems to be blaming us for letting her down. Still it's understandable in a way that she's pleased, gleeful. She's shown us she can manage perfectly well without our help. She may need social workers so badly that in a way she hates us all. Does she know how badly she needs us? Anyway, she must thoroughly distrust a newcomer like me and need to put on a show of pride in front of me.

"Oh good," I replied. "You must be very relieved that it won't now topple over on any of the children."

"Yes," she said, her glee fading.

Is she a manic depressive type? Quite clever of me to diagnose that if she is.

She evidently didn't want to enlarge on the subject so I asked, without very much interest, whether Walton himself had mended the cupboard. She looked at me as though I were insane.

"What, that Walton! – 'im ever mend anything? – not on your life!" she exclaimed. "'e's one o' them good for nothing niggers never ought to've left the jungle. 'twas Bert. 'e done it Friday morning."

She is annoying. What an absurd conversation.

I was suddenly so cross that I broke a casework rule: I argued with a Client.

"Not all coloured people are from jungles you know," I rejoined. "Lots are very nice people from big towns. And they come here to get work and so that they don't starve in their own countries."

Somewhat deflated though still sounding disgruntled, she replied:

"Well any road they don't seem to do no work when they gets 'ere – filling up the Assistance office all day so's a decent, 'ard working man like my Bert's got to wait there hours till they gets out."

I ruminated for a moment.

So Mr Carter mended the cupboard on Friday morning, a working day... Yet when I called before she said he was back at work. Is he unemployed again so soon? Or has she been lying all along and he's been out of work the whole time? I'll probe her.

"Mr Carter fixed the cupboard you say on Friday morning. Wasn't he at work then? – I thought he'd just got a new job," I said quite sternly, still feeling too cross to probe gently. Mrs Carter at once looked very distressed.

She may in a way hate social workers, yet can't bear us to disapprove of her. She must be ashamed, both about his unemployment and because I've seen through her lies about it.

All her defences down, in a half bleating, half sobbing voice she confessed:

"No 'e ain't got no job. Last job 'e 'ad were two months back. Worked in a bakery an' got the sack in three days for sassing the boss. 'e ain't no sticker, Bert ain't. Never was. Didn't never stick nothing longer'n three weeks." Tears trickled down her cheeks streaking through her make-up. Sobbing hard, she added, "'an me with me 'aimorrhages an' all."

It's my duty to console her.

I moved close to her, resolutely stretched out my hand and placed it on her forearm.

How long before she calms down enough for me to ask about her haemorrhages? Now the subject's cropped up again I must seize the opportunity to find out more about it... On the other hand, should I stick to the business of Mr Carter's unemployment? Though in that case she might take longer to stop crying.

For a moment I stood stiffly in silence beside her, embarrassed by her proximity.

Perhaps she finds my feeble attempt to comfort her annoying.

I was relieved when Kathy suddenly staggered into the room, clasping a carrier bag that was so bulky she could only just see over the top of it. Mrs Carter instantly quelled her tears, tightened her misery-slumped features and, in an only slightly choking voice, said:

"That's a good girl Kathy." Turning to me, she added, "She's been on a message – done the shopping at the corner shop."

Poor little thing – she's completely weighed down! Surely she's too young to be sent shopping? Or is it normal for toddlers in this sort of neighbourhood to be sent on such errands? Of course it does I suppose help train them to become useful, responsible citizens... Which reminds me – Willy. The main purpose of my visit is to try and do something about his behaviour... Still, seeing Kathy's here and he isn't perhaps I can put him off for a bit and try playing with Kathy. If I play with her successfully, as I did with Mary Kelly, it may help make up for all my blunders so far today with Mrs Carter.

Unfortunately Kathy was more like Betty than Mary. When I squatted down in front of her and said ingratiatingly:

"Hullo Kathy, how are you today?" her only response was to stare blankly at me. After a moment's pause I tried again, "You remember me don't you? – the lady who called to see your Mum the other day." But she still just stared. Whether she remembered me or not she clearly did not wish to renew the acquaintance.

Determined not to be thwarted, I gingerly placed my thumb under her chin, then wriggled two or three fingers about beneath it. Her only reaction was to dilate her eyes into an expression of mildly displeased surprise. Then, daringly, I thrust all my fingers quite strenuously into her hair.

Oh dear, how lank and sticky it is. And what shall I do next? Her expression's so forbidding that it would be inappropriate, even hypocritical, to rumple her hair affectionately. But if I just withdraw my fingers from her hair and stop touching her this might reinforce the rejected, unloved feeling which is apparently stunting her emotional development.

Mrs Carter watched balefully in silence for a few moments then remarked:

"Doctor reckons she's got impetigo."

I promptly withdrew my fingers, then instantly regretted doing so.

I shouldn't have done that. Mrs Carter will be insulted, and I've probably upset Kathy too. She may not be as apathetic and unresponsive as she seems – underneath she may well be very sensitive. All the same, Mrs Carter might have warned me a bit sooner about her impetigo and not just watched while I was probably catching it from her.

Luckily just then the door-bell rang. Mrs Carter sent Kathy to answer it. She returned accompanied by a woman in a round hat, bottle-green suit and flat shoes, carrying a brief-case.

She must be a social worker too. She could be about the same age as Miss Homer at St. Hugh's Hospital, but somehow she looks older – almost elderly. Her spuriously breezy manner however doesn't match her trim, prim appearance.

"Well, how's everything today, Mrs Carter," she said, smiling brightly. "No catastrophes I hope?" More seriously she added, "Indeed I do hope no crises have occurred that you might have wanted to get in touch with me about as for the last couple of days the Department's line's been out of order." Turning to me, she remarked, "Scandalous, isn't it, how long they take to repair important things like that these days."

Does she realise I'm a social worker too? Somehow I doubt it.

Turning back to Mrs Carter the woman enquired:

"Well, how's our plan for Willy working out then? What does

he think about giving the Carthage Street Club a try?" Not waiting for a reply, she continued, "It's just the club for him, I feel sure. Mr Ray, unlike so may club leaders, is all out to help lads who've been in trouble."

She must be Willy's Probation Officer. Surprising she's prepared to discuss her Client in front of a complete stranger...How different we must look: she all ladylike and me young and untidy. And compared with me she seems so self-assured. I'd better not let on I'm a social worker too. She'd be so contemptuous of me...Though I must say she's a bit prim and at the same time over-jolly – not like the others at Hunter Street.

But when presently Mrs Carter said:

"Well I'm sure I'm very grateful Miss Johnson," I was envious.

In a way I'd rather be called "Miss Green" than "Hilary" – I'd feel safer, more secure. It would help Mrs Carter to understand I'm a proper, paid, professional social worker. Being called "Hilary" makes me sort of almost a family friend, which I'm not – someone she can ask to do anything and everything for her.

Miss Johnson said:

"Well this is only meant to be a short visit. I just popped in because our phone's out of order in case you'd wanted to get in touch with me about anything. I'll look in again soon – though if anything does crop up be sure and let me know. They're bound to fix our line soon."

I was agreeably astonished when Mrs Carter replied:

"Thank you but I'm sure this lady'll 'elp out if anything 'appens like."

So she thinks more of me than of Miss Johnson, a superlatively trained Probation Officer!

Miss Johnson looked at me puzzled, and I, blushing, explained who I was.

"Oh, I didn't know your Agency was in touch with Mrs Carter at the moment," she responded.

Is she relieved? regretful? resentful? There may be some inter-agency rivalry.

Whatever her instant reaction however, she seemed delighted to enlighten me about Willy as we descended the stairs together a few minutes later. Apparently he had been put on probation about a month ago for stealing money left on doorsteps for the milkman. She knew nothing about the van theft I had witnessed and seemed very interested in my account of it.

Full of self-confidence after Mrs Carter's compliment and reassured by Miss Johnson's comradely manner, I dared to add a few opinions about Willy and the family as a whole. She seemed impressed.

"Thank you for telling me all this. Thank you very much indeed," she said quite effusively. "Much of this is quite new to me and your observations are most acute. Mrs Carter does indeed seem a singularly frustrated woman, and this may well affect the children's behaviour. I only wish we Probation Officers had time to work as closely with our cases as you folk do. We must work together on the family. I'll keep in touch with you about them and I hope you will with me, then perhaps we can really get somewhere."

I returned to the Agency full of pride. Surely Monica would be impressed when she heard I had won the confidence of such a highly skilled fellow caseworker?

Chapter 29

"I think," said Monica as we were finishing dinner, "that this might be a good moment, while we are all gathered together, to make a brief announcement – which I am most reluctant to have to make."

I'm sure she isn't.

"It is just this, and I want to get it over as quickly as possible so that the matter can be over and done with, for my own sake as well as for everyone else's peace of mind, since what I have to say is, as I'm sure you will realise, as painful for me to have to tell as it will be for you to learn." She paused.

Why can't she get to the point? Why be so ponderous?

"What I'm afraid I have to tell you," she resumed, "is that, most reluctantly, we shall soon have to say goodbye to one of our Probationers." As she paused again I was briefly panic-stricken.

Is it me after all, not Godfrey, who's getting the sack?

"Godfrey," she at last concluded, "will shortly be leaving us to engage in some other sort of work for which he will be better suited, better able to be himself, and which will more fully employ his not inconsiderable talents that, as he himself agrees, have not found full expression here with us." She stopped.

Why can't she just say straight out that he's no good? Why be so long-winded and hypocritical? In fact why make this pompous utterance at all? Everyone must know by now that he's leaving. She just likes periodically making weighty pronouncements, being dramatic. She's quite cruel. And I bet he didn't really agree.

There was a general murmur of regret. Godfrey's head was bent so I couldn't tell how he was reacting. The others too were either looking down at their plates or gazing away into the middle distance as though trying to detach themselves from the painful situation they themselves had helped to create. Only Monica appeared composed. She was looking straight at me.

Why's she staring at me like that? Is it because we're sitting opposite each other, or is she sending me some message – a warning?

"While we are gathered together like this as a group is there by any chance anything else anyone would like to raise?" she asked. "Anything personal, about group relations – not work or practical matters as we dealt with that at our meeting the other evening."

So she wants another group discussion.

After a short silence Ann said:

"Well yes, I suppose there is." Monica looked displeased.

Strange, I was wrong – she doesn't seem to want another discussion. So why invite one? Maybe just to change the subject, relieve the tension?

"Yes there is something I'd like to raise," she repeated. "It is a problem to do with personal relations. I don't know just quite how to put it, how to begin." She stopped.

How surprising. She usually seems so frank and to the point. It must be some very difficult problem.

Everyone (except Godfrey, who was immersed in gloom) looked at her attentively. "It's like this," she said slowly. "And as it's all so awkward and unpleasant and hard to know how to put without hurting anyone too much I hope you don't mind if I preface it a bit?" Again she stopped. Everyone but Godfrey looked keenly interested. One or two heads nodded and she resumed, "Yes, well, this is how I see it. Here we are, a group of very different personalities all trying to work and live together. The working together's difficult enough at times, but the living together's much harder. We have regular group meetings and so on and are always discussing everything very thoroughly so that we don't make the wrong decisions. We try to deal with anything disruptive that arises – don't we? – as we try to work as a unit, organically so to speak."

She's being extraordinarily long-winded and verbose.
What's she getting at?

The others began to look impatient rather than eager. "In short, what I'm trying to say is that we, as a group, being this kind of group, should always try and face up to facts about ourselves – even unpleasant ones. That's what you've always tried to get us to do, Monica, isn't it?" Monica nodded, and she resumed, "What I'm driving at is you, Ben – your behaviour. I'm sorry to have to say this, but I think the time has come to. You just can't go on carrying on the way you do."

By now she was speaking forcefully, almost fiercely. Ben looked startled; the others mystified. His surprise turned to indignation as she continued:

"It's your attitude towards the rest of us – towards us girls." She paused and everyone again looked exceedingly interested. "We're a mixed group," she went on. "Always patting ourselves on the back about how beautifully and platonically we get on together – though goodness knows why. But you, Ben, you cause a lot of unhappiness and can be emotionally most disruptive. Maybe you can't altogether help it, but you seem to feel you must chase one girl after another in the group." She glared at him. "Some of us can deal with you O.K. – Clara for instance, and you soon gave up with Gladys."

I wonder why?

"Though that's all hearsay to me – happened long before my time. But as far as I'm concerned, let's face it, you've never stopped making a dead set at me regardless of how discouraging I've been." Again she paused. By now Ben was glaring back at her. "But it's not me I'm worried about," she went on. "I can look after myself. It's Nell. She's so vulnerable, yet you simply play with her – use her as a sort of second string to fiddle flirtatiously with." Turning to Nell, she said, "Sorry, Nell, to have to go into all this. But it's high time someone did." Looking back at Ben steadily and reproachfully, she said, "I've found Nell in tears Ben – yes, in tears, and more than once. And even though she doesn't say why, we all know the reason perfectly well, don't we?" She glanced round at us all. "She loves you, Ben," she stated, "– if you know what that means. And you just play with her feelings." She had finished at last. She looked down at her plate.

After a brief silence Monica said quietly:

"Well Ben?" But before he could respond Nell burst out:

"That's bloody unfair Ann."

She must be very jealous of her, looking at her so ferociously.

"Ben's never led me on or led me to expect more than he's meant. I don't accept what you're saying at all – anyway not about him and me."

She's defending both him and herself. How shallow and fickle my feelings about Godfrey are compared with hers about Ben.

"Well Ben?" Monica repeated. He shrugged his shoulders and replied with forced casualness:

"Yes, of course it's true I like girls. Always have. Most fellows do – unless they're queer. And some girls more than others."

To my surprise Godfrey jerked himself out of his despondency and said:

"That's just not good enough. It's one thing to like girls, and some more than others; but it's quite another matter to be pointlessly cruel and gratuitously make some girl unhappy – especially a nice, defenceless girl like Nell." Unable even now to resist theorizing, he added, "Defenceless I mean because, as we all know, loving truly and deeply always means losing one's emotional defences. And you knew she loved you."

He's being exceedingly critical. Perhaps he's trying to get his own back on at least one of them for sacking him. Anyway, it's good that for once he can forget himself and his own troubles and worry about someone else…Odd, I seem to still care how he behaves. Is it because I, my fate, seems somehow bound up with his?

Ben didn't answer. Smirking at Nell seated opposite him, he

merely remarked with a chuckle:

"Oh, so we're lovers Nell are we! When did this happy event occur I wonder."

But nobody found his forced jocularity funny. Everyone looked at him intently, evidently expecting something more. Suddenly he rose abruptly from the table and left the room, whether in shame, embarrassment or anger I couldn't tell.

After a short silence Gladys ventured:

"Well it's a good thing isn't it to clear the air once in a while about our group relations and bring any personal problems out into the open?" She glanced anxiously round at us.

"Platitudes won't help just now," Monica rejoined brusquely.

*Why be so cutting? Has Gladys annoyingly assumed her
role, or is she punishing her for her very inoffensiveness?*

Echoing Gladys, she went on, "It is indeed important to raise and carefully consider any inter-personal problems and tensions that may arise. Ben will have to think over very carefully what has been said, but I don't feel we should continue discussing the matter in his absence. Anyway, since this is not a regular Group Meeting I think we should close the discussion for the moment and see how things work out."

We all left the table.

Chapter 30

I was half-way upstairs when Monica called out:

"Oh, Hilary, I wonder if you could spare me a few minutes." I went back down to her office. "Well, how did you get on at the Carters' this morning?" she asked.

*How does she know I went there? Did Ann tell her? If so,
did she report the rest of our conversation – tell her how
anxious I am about Willy and about how I'm getting on
here? I hope not. If she did, Godfrey may be right about
her being two-faced.*

"Oh, I think it all went all right thank you," I answered. On the spur of the moment I couldn't remember what had happened at the Carters'; it was blotted out by what had happened at dinner-time. Remembering next minute what a successful visit it had been, I was disappointed when Monica promptly changed the subject.

"I've looked over your casepapers. They seem competently written up, though occasionally a bit muddled and repetitious. You don't, for instance, need to describe a Client's illness three times over under separate headings. But I was sorry you were unable to offer more personal opinions and comments under 'General Trends'. This is the crucial part of case recording. It's where the caseworker suggests possible policies and approaches and is therefore infinitely more important than bare facts about the number of beds in the house and so on, isn't it?"

But the other day she said the exact opposite: stressed the importance of getting precise facts and figures. Very baffling.

I nodded.

"Yes, I suppose so," I assented. "I'll try and do that more in future. It wasn't that I didn't have any ideas about possible trends and policies."

Is that true?

"Just that I hadn't realised they were supposed to be written down in the casepapers, if you see what I mean." She probably didn't for she merely said:

"Mm," then changed the subject again. "Well now you've contacted various people since we last talked. There's been Mrs Kelly in hospital and your telephone calls to Mrs Carter's doctor and to the National Assistance Board. By the way, what happened with the Probation Department?"

"Their line was out of order," I replied. "But I did meet Miss Johnson, Willy's Probation Officer, when I was round at the Carters' this morning." Unfortunately I paused before continuing my narrative thus lost the chance of describing my successful visit.

"Yes I see," Monica broke in. "Now about Mrs Kelly – I gather she's due out of hospital tomorrow. I take it you'll be accompanying her and the baby home. Then your phone calls. You didn't manage to get much out of the Carters' doctor, did you? However, Mr Curtis was able to give you some useful information about the family."

Does she know him personally? I hope not. The better she knows officials like him the more she'll probably hear about all my blunders.

"Yes, he told me quite a lot of things," I assented. At last Monica gave me my opening.

"Well, what about this morning?" she asked. "Did you find out anything more from Mrs Carter?" At last I was able to give an account of my morning visit; but I couldn't tell whether Monica was impressed or even interested as all she said was:

"Yes, I see. But you didn't, I gather, manage after all this to find out much more about Mr Carter's employment pattern?"

"Well no," I replied. "I suppose not. Nothing except what she said about him being out of work at the moment. The Probation Officer arrived just as I was going to ask about this, so it made it difficult to go on pressing for details after that."

Monica nodded slightly, then appeared thoughtful.

Is she gathering herself together, getting up steam, to make some profound utterance? She could be hiding any slight approval she may feel about my success – sort of success – this morning. Perhaps she doesn't believe in praising Probationers in case it makes them lazy. Though of course she may not have been impressed by my morning's work anyway.

"Well now, Hilary," she said. "You have done a considerable number of things, made a number of contacts and had several interviews. I think the time has come to make some comment on your progress."

Again she paused. My anxiety mounted. I stared fixedly at some doodling on her scribbling-pad.

It's like a great spider in a web… Why can't she get on with it? Is she deliberately prolonging my suspense? Odd – I wanted to get Godfrey and Ann to tell me how they thought I was getting on, but now I don't want to hear Monica's views.

"It is only fair I think," she resumed, enunciating very clearly, "to tell you that we do feel just a trifle uncertain about you."

Is it a six- or seven-stranded cobweb?… Oh well, so that's how they feel about me – a relief in a way to know. But surely it's a bit soon for them to come to such a conclusion?

"The trouble is," she went on, "that your work is hindered by over-anxiety. Some degree of anxiety is to be expected of course. Indeed it would be wrong if you were not at all anxious – that was Godfrey's problem – over-confidence, too much self-assurance. In your case insecurity has been evident from the outset, both in your work and in your behaviour as a member of the group."

What's that got to do with it? We're discussing my work, not me as an individual or group member.

"You're in a state of perpetual slight tension, which inevitably affects your Clients and your relationship with them. Take Betty for example. If you had been able to relax more with her you would, I am sure, have managed better with her, wouldn't you? Not that she's an easy child of course, but that's the crux of the matter – none of our Clients are easy people. That's why they're our Clients." She stopped and looked hard at me.

"Yes, I see," I responded.

"Then take Charly Dale," she pursued. "You were so keyed up when he phoned that you simply didn't hear what he said, did you? You passed on the message that his wife had just had a baby. In fact she had just lost it. It was still-born."

But I did listen. It wasn't my fault he was unintelligible.

"Oh dear, I'm dreadfully sorry," I lied. "But he is awfully hard to understand, isn't he? Hasn't he got some speech defect?"

"Well yes, he has," she conceded. "That is so. But there you are you see, Hilary. This is just another case in point – your need to be defensive, which is a form of insecurity. It comes out all the time." Allowing a note of sympathy to replace the triumph, she added, "Is there anything that we – I or any of us – can do to help you over this? You've only to ask. Perhaps some quite deep-seated trouble is making you over-anxious and defensive? If we could bring it to the surface and deal with it you might become a good caseworker. You've plenty of intelligence and intellectual capacity for understanding other people."

So she expects me to try and describe all my personal problems and anxieties does she? Well I won't. I'm not going to let myself be turned into a Client, and no amount of flattery will get me to.

I made no response. This may have annoyed Monica for she resumed:

"I realise no one can be free of anxiety and tension all the time. However, I'm afraid there is a tendency for people with quite serious problems to take up social work as a form of

134

sublimation. They believe that in solving others' problems they can solve their own. But it isn't true. No one's problems are solved, least of all their Clients'. Indeed they may do their Clients serious harm." She paused.

> *How confusing. Ann said exactly the opposite. Who am I to believe?*

Sounding a shade less severe, she went on, "You, Hilary, clearly have certain problems that need to be tackled. However, your work has not been without merit. All the same, you will need to become a great deal more relaxed and capable of making decisions and acting on your own initiative. We shall be watching closely to see how you progress."

Chapter 31

Back in the General Office I tried in vain to concentrate on writing up my morning visit. The room was empty at first, then Gladys entered. I was so worried and depressed that, without weighing the wisdom of my words, I said:

"I know it's rather a direct question, Gladys, but of course what's happened to Godfrey's upset me rather. I mean, I feel a bit, you know, worried about myself now. I'm wondering how people, well, think I'm getting on?"

Choosing not to regard this as a question, Gladys responded in her hushed tone:

"Yes, it's terrible for us all. It's always awful when something like this has to happen. And it must be worst for you." She smiled kindly at me.

> *Has she mistaken my selfish anxiety for concern about Godfrey?*

"Yes, well, as you can imagine," I persisted, "It's made me sort of wonder about myself. What's your opinion of me, my work, so far? How've I been getting on? You don't think the same thing's going to happen to me as Godfrey do you?"

> *Surely even she can hardly misunderstand or evade quite such a direct question?*

"Oh no love, of course not. You needn't worry about that," she replied.

Is she being honest or merely trying to reassure me?

After a moment's silence she added, "It's really bad luck for you – such a thing happening just now when you're so new here yourself."

I tried again:

"Yes, but can you give me some idea about my own progress? Am I doing too badly? – worse than most Probationers?"

"Well, love," she responded slowly, "there've been ups and downs, but on the whole I'd say you've coped quite well with the Clients I've seen you with – though of course I've only seen you with the Kellies. You seemed by and large to relate quite well to them. But you must ask Monica this sort of question. She could give you a much better, fairer answer than me."

I gave up and returned to my report.

Presently Ann entered the office and said:

"Oh there you are Glad. Where's Ben? Monica wants us in her office about something?" They both left the room.

Yet another exclusive little meeting?

The front-door bell rang, then rang again. As everyone else was evidently busy or out I decided I'd better answer it.

A boy of about thirteen stood on the doorstep.

"I've come for the clothes," he stated.

"Oh yes," I replied, trying to size him up.

He looks too sturdy and well dressed to belong to a problem family. But appearances can be deceptive. He may be deeply disturbed or grossly delinquent.

"Yes, of course, the clothes," I added slowly – having learnt from the others the technique of spinning out and making the most of any brief pause at the beginning of an encounter, thus gaining time in which to attempt a condensed appraisal of the individual confronting one.

Who is he? What clothes does he mean?

After a second or two I asked, "Which clothes? Who are they for? Who're you?"

He looked surprised.

"Jim Green," he replied. "Come for me Uncle's clothes 'as been promised 'im for 'is new job."

"Who here works with Mr Green?" I asked.

Though I think I'll try and deal with this myself so as not to disturb the others. It will show initiative.

136

"Mr Green?" he said, looking baffled for a moment, then added, "Oh, I ain't come about me Dad. 'e don't know no one 'ere. It's me Uncle Charly – Dale's 'is name."

But surely Charly Dale is supposed to have started his job a day or two ago? So why's he still not got the new clothes for it? Will I ever hear the end of Charly Dale and his new job and clothes?

"Oh Charly Dale," I said. "He wants a coat and shoes doesn't he? And an overcoat? And what size shoes does he wear?"

"Dunno," he replied. "But I can tell 'ow big when I sees 'em."

"Well you'd better come in and see what we've got," I responded; and we went upstairs to the store-cupboard in the attic.

Annoyingly the door was locked.

Monica's probably got the key. I'll have to interrupt their discussion after all.

Then I noticed a key lying half hidden behind a box in the corner. Cheered by this iota of good luck, I said quite warmly:

"Come along in then and we'll see what we can find."

The store-cupboard was an enlarged cubbyhole, crammed with a higgledy-piggledy assortment of battered shoes, tattered frocks and underwear and grimy, smelly coats and trousers. We rummaged around for a few minutes, then he held up a threadbare, greenish sports-jacket, slightly torn at one leather-patched elbow, and stated:

"This'll do."

"All right – I expect it's all right if you take that one," I responded.

Why's he so terse, as though he's conferring a favour on us by deigning to accept one of our coats?

"Now for the shoes."

We continued to ransack the cupboard. From time to time I produced some fairly water-tight looking pair of shoes and said:

"What about these?" Every time he shook his head. Eventually he announced:

"These'll do," holding up a pair of mud-encrusted boots.

"But they're football boots!" I expostulated.

"They'll do," he repeated, and scrambled out of the cubbyhole, trampling and tearing some items of underwear in the process.

"But football boots won't do for work," I said.

*Absurd, to give him football boots for a new job – or is
he going on a building site? Anyway, I'm not going to let
a mere child browbeat me. I'll prove I'm not weak willed
– that Monica's wrong.*

I handed him the first fairly sound pair of men's walking-shoes
I unearthed and said firmly, "I think these will be better. Give
him these."

I locked the cupboard door and we went downstairs in silence.
He thanked me gruffly as I held the door open for him.

*He looks awfully sullen. Did he plan to keep the football
boots for himself? Anyhow, I've managed on my own to
deal efficiently with this situation.*

I was about to return upstairs when they all emerged from
Monica's office.

"Oh Ben," I said, "Charly Dale's nephew's just been for his
coat and shoes for his new job. I knew he was supposed to have
them so we got a passable sports coat for him and some good,
strong shoes. But it was incredible – the boy wanted to take a
pair of muddy old football boots."

"Oh, come for the clothes at last have they?" Ben replied, not
sounding very interested, then added, "Did you give him the
football boots?"

"Of course not," I answered. "I thought he needed ordinary
shoes for work. I got him some ordinary leather walking-shoes."

"Well he could have worn the football boots to work couldn't
he?" he said with a merry laugh. "Keen on football, our Charly
– anyway, you might have given him both pairs."

*So after all I did the wrong thing – or anyhow not the
right thing.*

"I'm sorry," I replied. "I didn't know he needed football boots
– played football." Ben guffawed and exclaimed:

"Charly Dale – football!" He glanced round at the others,
inviting them to share this esoteric joke.

*Probably he doesn't play football at all. Ben's just making
fun of me. How aggravating it all is.*

Sounding deliberately casual, I dismissed the subject:

"Oh well, I'm afraid I know nothing about Charly Dale or his
recreations or job – if he's even got one. I just thought you'd
like to hear his clothes have been collected at last." Turning to
Monica, I added, "By the way, here's the store-cupboard key. I

found it lying on the floor outside. I don't know where it's kept."
I handed her the key, and she rewarded me:

"Oh good. How observant of you. I'd been wondering where it had got to. But for you we might have had to force the lock." She smiled at me.

Is she trying to make amends for her earlier sternness?

But by now I was impervious to consolation. I was so tired of them all that I decided to spend the evening alone in my room playing Beethoven late quartets.

Chapter 32

Next morning I set off for St. Hugh's Hospital equipped with an assortment of baby-clothes, only to learn that Mrs Kelly had gone home the day before. I cycled off, debating whether to conceal my mistake – if it were a mistake – from Monica; whether to fabricate an account of accompanying Mrs Kelly home for the casepaper and risk Monica's discovering it was all lies. Turning into Olivia Terrace, seeing the two rows of dismal, decrepit houses lining the street, I realised with shame I had been worrying so much about myself that I had hardly thought about Mrs Kelly and her problems.

Did she get home all right on her own? How has she been coping with the baby? All those instructions Gladys gave me for her…Is she feeding and bathing the baby properly and has she got it some sort of bed?

I banged on the cracked front-door. Mrs Kelly's voice called out:

"'oo's there?"

"It's me, Hilary, from Hunter Street," I called back. "Can I come in?"

The living-room was as gloomy and cave-like as before compared with the sunny street outside; yet somehow it was different from last time I was there: less savagely garish and squalidly cosy: drearier; more like a cavern than a cave. This morning the atmosphere was both stale and chilly. The flickering coal fire had become a heap of ashes, and there was a depressing morning-after feeling about the room.

139

As before, Mrs Kelly was seated hunched and monolithic in her armchair on the hearth. I was pleasantly surprised when she greeted me with zest. She smiled at me, the smile expanding and bursting into a throaty chuckle as she spoke.

"'ere we are then, 'ome again you see, lovey," she announced. Wondering what was so funny, I smiled back. "An' 'is Lordship 'ere on 'is throne an' in 'is palace an' all," she went on. She indicated a battered, hood-less pram over in the corner. Presumably it contained the baby.

Why's she so pleased? I don't understand. She didn't want another baby, yet here she is, delighted with it even though it's the wrong sex. She's positively merry, not dull and dismal after all. Well anyway it's refreshing to find a Client in good spirits for once.

Infected by her mood, I exclaimed:

"Oh, I must have a look at him and see how he's taken to his new throne!"

For a second I was quite excited about the new baby itself, although as a rule all I felt about new-born infants was a mixture of boredom and mild revulsion.

Where are the other children? But I won't ask about them just now.

I approached the pram.

I must pay some convincing compliment.

The baby was certainly unprepossessing. There it lay, beneath a thin, greyish blanket. Although less than a week old, its peaked features looked strangely elderly. Its vacuous, unfocused eyes suggested senility rather than infancy, and its red skin made it distastefully raw looking. The unwholesome smell emanating from the pram reminded me of Gladys's instructions.

I must find out if she's got something to bath it in, and ask if she's boiling the nappies and sterilizing the milk-bottle regularly.

"My, isn't he a beauty!" I lied, then added, "By the way, here are some clothes and things Gladys gave me to give you for him." I presented her with the parcel of clothing. Rather surprisingly, she did not at once open it. "How are you managing with him?" I asked. "Gladys tells me that in the past your mother used to help you out quite a bit over looking after your babies."

My question instantly dispelled her good humour. Suddenly

140

woebegone, she replied with an ominous throb in her voice:

"Me mother's dead an' gone. Honest to God, 'ilary lovey, I don't know what to do with 'im. I ain't to blame, swear to God I ain't. But 'e'll die, won't 'e? – poor little bugger – swear to God 'e will."

I was taken aback by this switch in mood.

Do unintelligent people's moods keep changing abruptly?
– first joy then utter gloom. If so, why? Are intelligence
and emotional stability somehow connected?

"Oh, it's surely not that bad," I responded, but Mrs Kelly went on:

"Just don't know what to do, I don't. Swear to God 'e'll die. Will you 'elp me with 'im lovey?"

Oh dear, am I sounding too comforting, reminding her
of her mother? Obviously she wants me to take charge of
the baby like her mother did. But should I? I'm sure she's
got a great welter of mixed up, contradictory feelings
about her mother as she's been so dependent on her all
her life. If I let her turn me into a mother-figure I'll be
completely out of my depth. Still, I must be positive – show
Monica I've got some initiative. And I simply mustn't let
anything disastrous happen to this baby. It's one of my
Clients…I think I'll risk turning into her mother-figure.
I'll give her all the advice I can – it won't be much anyway
– never mind what the textbooks say about never being
"directive" with a Client. I'll even try and give her some
practical help.

"Yes, all right, we'll see what we can do together shall we?" I replied. To forestall the bout of weeping that seemed imminent, I proceeded to ask a string of questions.

"Now I wonder what arrangements you've been able to make for him?" I said. Adopting a merry tone to relieve her gloom, I went on, "I see he's got his throne." She looked blank so I hastily amended, "– his pram, I mean. But about his feeding, you are keeping his bottle sterilized aren't you? – filling it up with boiling water every time after he's used it so as to kill any germs?" Lest she thought I were casting aspersions on the cleanliness of her house, I added, "I mean babies are so apt to pick up just any germs that happen to be flying about anywhere, so you can't be too careful."

"'e don't 'ave no bottle – don't need one," she responded. I was baffled. All babies needed bottles.

"Yes, I see," I lied, and was silent for a moment.

I'd better not ask why – she'd think me stupid.

I stood still looking at her: studying her wispy, greyish hair, still in curlers; then the tough fibre sprouting from a mole on her neck just above a slight tear in the shapeless navy-blue dress, within which her pendulous breasts hung heavily down. Suddenly it dawned on me why this baby did not need a bottle. With a short, involuntary laugh, I exclaimed.

"No, of course he doesn't. What was I thinking of!" Changing the subject, I went on, "But there's the question of nappies. You are boiling them regularly so as to kill any germs, aren't you?"

I'm sure she isn't, but asking questions seems a good, indirect, non-directive way of giving advice – not too bossy.

I was disconcerted when she promptly replied:

"Yes, 'ilary, boiling 'em regular I am."

I very much doubt it, but I mustn't let the matter drop.
The baby might get very ill – entiritis…

But as I could think of nothing to say I switched to another, equally vital topic.

"What about bathing him?" I asked. "Can you manage that all right?"

"Yes thank you lovey," she replied. The time had come to risk offending her, so I pursued:

"Yes, well, you can't bath babies as young as he is too often you know. Might it be good to give him another one?"

After all, in the casepapers I've had to read the workers seem from time to time to have helped their Clients in practical ways – helped them to cook, make clothes, scrub floors. Though if I give her this sort of practical help may she get dangerously – unhealthily – emotionally dependent on me? Still, I simply must win Monica's approval by doing something decisive and positive.

"Would you like me to bath him?" I asked. "Or rather, shall we do him together?" She welcomed the suggestion.

But it soon appeared that I was going to be left to do the job on my own. I asked for something to bath the baby in. Mrs Kelly replied incoherently, then just sat back smiling, leaving me to

142

hunt around for a suitable receptacle. She may not have immediately understood what I was doing. Presently, however, she remarked:

"'s gone. We borrowed it to me sister-in-law when she 'ad 'er fourth. Never got it back – pan for bathing 'im, I mean." I resisted the temptation to remind her of her claim to have bathed the baby already. Tired of vacillating, I said briskly:

"Well in that case I think we'd better buy a bowl or something to wash him in." She promptly said she couldn't afford one.

"Very well then, I'll lend you the money," I replied (even though caseworkers were probably not meant to make loans to their Clients). "You must at least have a bowl to bath him in." Recalling something I had read in one of the casepapers, I added, "We can make some arrangement whereby you can repay me, can't we? – on Mr Kelly's pay-day perhaps." But she just responded:

"'im? Won't get nothing out of 'im."

I left the house and set off in search of an ironmonger's. Before long I returned with a fairly cheap, capacious washing-up bowl. If only the baby never grew I would not have to face the problem of how to bath him when he was too big for this container.

"Here it is. It'll do, won't it?" I announced, then was instantly deflated when Mrs Kelly stated:

"'tain't no use. Ain't got no coal."

What's coal got to do with it? Oh, of course, they've got no hot running water. We'll have to heat up cold water from the tap in the back-yard.

"I don't really know just what we can do then," I answered, feeling too discouraged to try to cope with yet another problem.

My very despair seemed to galvanize her; for, after a short silence, she suggested:

"They'd likely let you 'ave a spot o' warm water over at bath-'ouse. 's down the second opening." I brightened up.

"That's an idea," I replied. "We can have a try anyway."

In future I'll let her solve her own problems. The less other people do for her the more responsible and self-reliant she should become. Caseworkers are supposed to try and make their Clients responsible and self-reliant.

It took me some time to find the bath-house. Mrs Kelly's "second opening" turned out to be the third on the right on the opposite side of the street running parallel to Olivia Terrace. Nearly half an hour later, I staggered back into Mrs Kelly's living-room, hugging in my aching arms a half-filled basin of water, by then only luke-warm. I also had a piece of carbolic soap, thoughtfully provided by the bath-house supervisor.

"Here it is at last. Now, on with the bath," I said, cheerful despite the weariness of my strained arms and the itchiness of my splashed shins. I set the bowl down on the floor, and Mrs Kelly rewarded me by responding:

"My, you're a one, 'ilary!"

"I think we'd better do him on the table," I said. Swiftly and methodically I cleared away a clutter of greasy plates, tea-slopped cups, apple cores and crumpled paper. Now I felt self-confident: able to be brisk and practical.

I remained undaunted when, a few minutes later, I was faced with the distasteful task of actually bathing the writhing, whimpering infant. I forced myself not to think about what I was doing as I groped in its filth-caked cavities, and tried not to notice the appalling diminutiveness of its member. All the same, I handled it gingerly, afraid of inadvertently breaking or dislocating one of its fragile limbs or digits or letting its head drop back with a brittle snap.

What impression am I making on her? She's just standing there watching, not helping. I'm sure she's scornful of my clumsiness.

When at last the baby was bathed and back in the battered pram I said:

"Well I'd better be off now."

There's still heaps to discuss with her, but surely, after doing all this, I'm entitled to shelve it all for the moment?

"You'll know how to bath him yourself next time, won't you?" I added.

It's time I stopped being a nanny and tried some further actual casework.

She didn't answer. Instead she whined:

"When'll you be back lovey? Honest to God 'ilary, I can't get along without you. Honest to God I can't."

Gratified by this beseeching and relieved to learn she didn't despise me for my gauche handling of the baby, I was in a good mood when I returned to the Agency, proud of my morning's work.

At dinner-time I told the others what I had done, but their response was disappointing and baffling. Gladys and Ann exchanged swift, cryptic glances; then Gladys bowed her head slightly and lowered her eyes as though for some reason she were embarrassed or ashamed. Ann regarded me intently. After a brief pause, her voice infused with almost exaggerated kindness, she said:

"Yes, you do seem to have done a good morning's work with Mrs Kelly, Hilary." Then Nell, usually so reticent and enigmatic, remarked equally kindly:

"Yes, and Eva Kelly called when you were out or busy or something yesterday evening – sorry I forgot to tell you – and she couldn't say enough about how Mr Kelly had been raving about you, saying what a nice, clever person you are."

I was perplexed.

Why're they both being so kind? It all sounds a bit forced
– almost as if they're trying to reassure me. But why? For
once, just now, I don't need reassuring.

I glanced at Monica to see if her expression provided a clue to the puzzle. She was observing me very closely.

Chapter 33

I settled down to writing up and mulling over my reports. I felt quite relaxed and even started to form some tentative casework policies for my Clients. After I had been working for about an hour Ann came into the office and said:

"Hilary, Monica wants to see you." Her eyes were wide and glittering inexplicably.

Good. She probably wants to congratulate me on my visit
to the Kellies' – make up for not doing so at dinner.

But when I entered her office she did not at once look up from some document she was studying. I hovered uncertainly in front of her desk.

Shall I sit down or wait till she notices me? Not an
auspicious reception.

After a few moments she pushed the document aside and looked up. It lay at a slight angle so I could see my name on it.

*It must be that paper about me I saw when I was hunting
for the visiting cards – only there's quite a lot written on
it.*

"Do sit down Hilary," she said. I obeyed, leaning forward
somewhat tensely, alarmed by her ultra-kind tone and smile. She
switched off the smile, picked up the sheet of paper and, looking
hard at me, said:

"As I explained to you yesterday, we, the Senior Caseworkers,
do regularly assess the progress of any Probationer." She paused,
and my apprehension increased. "Indeed," she went on, "we
attempt an initial appraisal quite soon after a Probationer has
started and has visited one or two families, thus enabling some
progress assessment. We feel it is useful to make this kind of
early judgement as it provides a starting point, some sort of
indicator, for later assessments." Again she paused, looking
straight at me.

I'm back at school, facing a series of exams.

She stopped staring at me and appeared to be reading the
paper about me again.

*Now I'm a client. She's reading up my casepaper. As far
as I can see it's all neatly set out under separate headings.*

"Yes I see," I said, and waited for her to continue.

"Furthermore," she resumed, replacing the paper on the desk,
"we put some of our observations in writing. This means we can
maintain a form of progress record – which is useful, both for
us and for the Probationer concerned." I nodded.

Is she going to let me read their observations about me?

She put the document away in a drawer. Leaning forward
slightly over her desk and again regarding me searchingly, she
said:

"As I intimated yesterday, Hilary, we are all just a trifle troubled
about you. We, the senior caseworkers, had a little meeting
yesterday to discuss your first week's work."

*So that was what they were talking about when I was
sorting out Charly Dale's work clothes. That accounts for
their odd reaction, or lack of reaction, at dinner when I
told them about my Kelly visit.*

"We make a practice of talking over a newcomer's work at the
end of his or her first week as this can become the starting point
for further discussions later – the yardstick whereby we all,

including of course the Probationer, can judge what progress has been made."

I caught sight of the scribbling-pad with the spider-like doodle on it and felt briefly indignant.

Why should I be made to feel, be, like a fly caught and devoured by this Agency? Or is it just Monica who's the spider? After all, I did do quite well at the Kellies' this morning. I may in fact have saved the baby's life – I, who know next to nothing about babies.

I relaxed on my chair, crossed my knees in a composed fashion and remarked a trifle tartly:

"But that's a bit soon surely? – I mean, isn't it rather, well, soon, after only a week, to tell how someone is getting on?"

Laboriously she responded:

"As I explained, Hilary, this early appraisal is a means of achieving some sort of indicator, basis, for future appraisals. We all, including the Probationer himself, find this initial assessment exceedingly valuable. You might say it is a kind of starting point for further training."

Now I feel like a potential race-horse.

"Although," she went on "a caseworker's approach and techniques may improve beyond recognition as time goes on – indeed, it is essential that they do – nonetheless, the groundwork is there from the beginning; the potential can become clear within a week. Much is revealed by the Probationer's first encounter with a Client." She assumed a slightly ominous expression.

My first such encounter was with Betty…

"I see," I said again – although actually I didn't.

Surely it's unjust to start assessing newcomers so soon, before they've had a proper chance to demonstrate their capabilities?

Perhaps I looked somewhat sullen, for Monica, speaking more briskly, resumed:

"You may not fully agree with this procedure; however, our experience over the years indicates it is invaluable." She stopped.

So when's she going to tell me their assessment of me?

She may have sensed my resentment and in her turn felt suddenly irritated and disinclined to prolong the discussion for, still speaking quite briskly, she said:

"To come to the point then, Hilary. We have now, as I say, had a formal discussion about your first week's work here, and our general conclusion is much as I intimated yesterday. We feel there is a spark – seed if you like – there, but that you have a long way to go before it can come to fruition and that your first task must be to face up to your own basic personal problems. For if you cannot succeed in doing this, we are a little doubtful, even at this very early stage, whether you will ever find that you are quite fitted for this work. It may be early days, but the indications are there, the writing is on the wall." She stopped briefly, then added, "Any of us will, of course, be only too glad at any time to do all we can to help you over your difficulties and give you any training and advice you may need."

Why does she have to keep on about me sorting out my problems? I thought I was here to help other people solve theirs. Anyhow, I haven't got any particularly serious problems. Still, I'd better not say so. It would be wise to try and seem humble. And she says I can ask for advice at any time.

Hoping to extract a fraction of reassurance, if not positive praise (for surely my morning's work with Mrs Kelly had been moderately successful), I said cautiously:

"I wonder whether it might possibly be possible to give me some kind of general idea whether I set about things in, well, more or less the right sort of way at the Kellies' this morning? It would be very helpful to have just some sort of idea about this."

But Monica, glancing at her watch and rising from her chair, merely responded:

"I, we, would have to give very careful consideration to that before venturing an opinion, Hilary. Our initial appraisal of you and the written observations about your work to date cover the period up to today. We had our progress meeting about you yesterday. This means that at this stage it is only your work up to yesterday that we are commenting on." She took her coat off a peg. "Don't worry, Hilary," she said, smiling kindly as she held open the door for me. "There will be plenty of time for much further discussion with you about your problems and progress; but now I have to go out."

I returned to the General Office. I felt flat and cross, disinclined even to pretend to work – anyway, what work was there to do at the moment?

No one was in the office, so I drifted aimlessly around the room, picking up and putting down the one-eared toy polar bear, pointlessly examining the city map on the wall and vaguely speculating yet again about the picture of the urinating man on the window. I stared out of the window. All at once I heard in my head what might become the first few bars of the slow movement of a cello concerto. I had never before attempted to compose anything so ambitious, but now I decided to have a try. When I got a musical idea I had to put it down on paper immediately, otherwise I usually lost it irretrievably. Not caring whether anyone came in and found me obviously not even pretending to work, I sat down and began to draft my composition on the back of an old mimeographed memo. I remained undisturbed until nearly tea-time, when Ann came into the office.

"Hullo Hilary, how are you getting on?" she asked brightly – although she must have known quite well I was doing badly. Observing that I appeared to be drawing something, she came over to see what it was. I blushed. I did not have time to cover up the paper.

"What is it?" she asked with interest. "It's not a drawing is it – an abstract or something?"

"No well not exactly," I answered. "Actually it's sort of a piece of music – you know, just a vague idea for a theme; the beginning of something maybe." I hated being watched while trying to compose and was invariably embarrassed when obliged to try to explain what I was doing. Ann looked at me in wonder.

"My, you're a dark horse Hilary!" she said. "I never knew we had a composer among us. Monica – no one – told us you were musical. Do tell me, how do you set about composing something."

Good – she's impressed. But really, they're all supposed to be so perceptive! They've been discussing and dissecting me for hours on end yet they don't seem to know one of the most important things about me – me and music – even though I put something about it in my application.

I was spared from having to try to answer as just then Clara suddenly appeared in the doorway and said:

"Mrs Owens is downstairs in the Quiet Room, Ann. She's got

no food in the house or something and wants some money."

After tea I felt I just must get away from the Agency and everything to do with it. I didn't even want to stay in and work on the cello concerto – someone was sure to interrupt me. One of the Carters or Kellies might call. The practice at the Agency was for people to take it in turns to be "on duty" during the evenings and at weekends: to answer the door and telephone and cope with any crises that might occur, even if they were to do with someone else's Client. But in reality, if the caseworker concerned were in, even if not "on duty", he or she invariably dealt with the situation. The only way to be absolutely sure not to have to cope with some emergency out of working hours was simply not to be on the premises. So I went off to a concert on my own.

Chapter 34

When I came down to breakfast next morning only Gladys was in the dining-room.

"Oh dear," she said as soon as I appeared. "It was extremely unfortunate you were out yesterday evening – not that you were supposed to be in or anything. But it's just a pity you weren't as you've now got the Kellies and there was a bit of a crisis." She paused expectantly.

"Oh dear," I echoed.

Thank goodness I went out.

"What happened? What a nuisance I wasn't in seeing they're now my family."

In a hushed, rushed tone, as if no one else should overhear what she was saying, even though only I was present, she replied:

"Well it was like this you see love. Eva came round at about seven, quite hysterical. It seems that Mr Kelly, who's been off on one of his bouts again, as you know" (I didn't) "suddenly returned and found Mrs Kelly had had the baby and that it was a boy, which he didn't want. So he beat her up." She paused, then resumed dramatically, "You know, gave her two black eyes and a real punching all over. It was terrible. She was in a shocking state when I got round there – black and blue all over. I went round straight away of course, as you weren't in, and left Ben in charge here. And I made her a cup of tea and put the baby to bed and she was shaking all over and quite hysterical, talking about seeking refuge in the Salvation Army Hostel. He's beaten her up before, but never that badly. I only hope she's got no broken bones. Of course he'd threatened to do her in if she had a boy; but, you know, he's apt to make wild statements and threats, so it doesn't do to take them too seriously."

She paused. I couldn't think of an appropriate response. "How dreadful," I said weakly, then added, "So what happened next? What's the situation now?"

"Well," she resumed, still breathily excited, "I managed to persuade her not to leave home – though she did say he'd threatened to kill her when he got back from the pub – he'd gone out again before I arrived – but of course, as I said, he's said that sort of thing to her so often before you can't take it really seriously."

"No, I suppose not," I replied dubiously.

She's probably right. She's worked with them so long she must know what would be for the best. Still, if Mr Kelly's beaten his wife up that badly shouldn't she really have gone to hospital, at least for the night? Though if she had, who would have looked after the children? Maybe Gladys should have stayed at their home all night – or would that have been breaking rules, been contrary to Agency policy? How do caseworkers deal with crises like this? Such a fearful responsibility…How lucky I'd decided to go out yesterday evening.

"So anyway I stayed with her for quite a while," Gladys went on. "Trying to calm her down, you know. And Mr Kelly didn't come back while I was there. I'd taken some aspirin and dettol and cotton wool round with me in case she was, well, wounded or something. But she wasn't – only very badly bruised and shaken as far as I could tell. So when she'd had the tea and aspirin and seemed calmer I went. I told her you'd be round first thing in the morning to see how she is and help see to the baby and everything."

But shouldn't she have sent for the doctor, not just given her tea and aspirin? But I'd better not say so. Shall I ask

*her to come with me to their house? It seems a bit feeble
– still this is a crisis. I mustn't risk doing the wrong thing.
People might even die – the baby, Mrs Kelly, the other
children.*

I decided to chance seeming ineffective – after all, hadn't
Monica told me to ask for help and advice whenever I felt I
needed it.

"I suppose, Gladys," I asked, "you wouldn't – I mean would
it be possible for you to come with me this time, as, well, it all
sounds pretty serious, and I'm not yet terribly experienced?"

"I'd love to, love," she replied, "only I simply can't this
morning. Tommy Davis is up in court and I promised I'd be there
so that he wouldn't feel so insecure. I can't let him down. It
would be a kind of betrayal – but I'm sure you'll manage very
well, love. You've done very well with the Kellies so far."

*Then why's my first week's progress report so bad?
Perhaps they weren't really all so damning about me as
Monica made out – I don't understand.*

"Anyway," Gladys concluded, "I'm sure you'll find the worst
is over now. I managed to calm Mrs Kelly, and Mr Kelly has
probably just gone off again, and everything will be back to
normal – as normal as it ever is with the Kellies."

As soon as I had finished my breakfast I cycled off to the
Kellies'. I arrived to find a cluster of people on the pavement
outside their front-door. An ambulance and two police cars were
parked in front of the house. Gladys must have been wrong:
disaster had plainly befallen.

Some policemen seemed to be in charge, preventing other
people from entering the house. I didn't know what to do. In a
sense the Kellies were my responsibility – but not officially, for
the Hunter Street Agency was voluntary, not run by the
Corporation. I propped my bicycle against a wall and joined the
group on the pavement, trying to gather what had happened
from overheard scraps of conversation.

I had been there only a few moments when Mr Kelly was
marched handcuffed through the front-door, flanked by two
policemen. They went off in one of the police cars. Almost
immediately afterwards ambulance drivers appeared carrying
two loaded stretchers. Both bodies – one large and one small –
were covered. Then another policeman and a policewoman

152

came out of the house accompanied by Eva, Mary and the rest of the Kelly children. They all crowded into the other police car and drove off.

After repeatedly questioning the people standing around, I eventually gathered that Mr Kelly had stayed out all night and not returned home till about an hour before I myself arrived on the scene. No one seemed to know where he had been. When he had got back, apparently, he and Mrs Kelly had immediately had a very noisy argument. They had raged so loudly at each other that their next door neighbours had overheard. One of them had gone to the house to see what was happening. She had found Mrs Kelly slumped, apparently dead, on the floor, bleeding profusely from stab wounds, and Mr Kelly swaying drunkenly in the middle of the room, brandishing a bread-knife and still in a frenzy. Before the neighbour had had time to try to stop him he had roughly shoved screaming Mary out of his way, marched over to the pram and, bawling repeatedly:

"Bastard! fucking little bleeding bastard!" had picked the baby up by the legs and bashed it several times against the wall. By then more neighbours, disturbed by the din, had arrived on the scene. One of them had quickly found a police constable in a nearby street. All this had occurred less than half an hour before I arrived.

I returned to the Agency, went straight to Monica's office and reported as clearly and concisely as possible what I had seen and heard. Monica promptly telephoned the police, who confirmed the story.

Shocked though I was by what had happened, yet I felt quite pleased with myself over my handling of the situation. I had turned up punctiliously on the Kellies' doorstep within an hour of hearing from Gladys what had occurred the previous evening. Obviously it was not my fault that I had arrived after the event – although even if I had arrived before, it was exceedingly unlikely that I could have done anything to prevent the tragedy. Had I tried to stop Mr Kelly, he would very likely have attacked me too. I had found out what had happened and had immediately given Monica an accurate report. If anyone were to blame it was Gladys for having misjudged the gravity of the situation the evening before. Indeed, shortly after the police had confirmed her story, I had the temerity to remark to Nell and

Ann up in the General Office:

"Poor Gladys – she must feel especially terrible, having worked so long with the Kellies and making the mistake of not getting her to leave home last night."

I feel quite proud of myself – superior to Gladys. She may be Senior Caseworker, but nevertheless, unintentionally and indirectly, she has been, in a sense, responsible for two deaths.

"Yes, it's simply terrible," Ann responded, and Nell echoed:

"It's the worst thing that's happened since I came here." I couldn't tell what they thought about Gladys's behaviour.

I didn't get the chance to talk to Gladys herself just then as Monica immediately despatched her to the police station to see the Kelly children and make arrangements for them to be taken into care.

"You see, love," Gladys hurriedly explained as she was about to set off, "we feel that in a situation like this, where the children need all the emotional support they can get, that I know the family so well and you have only just taken them on so that the children haven't quite got used to you yet, that, well, it might be best if I went to see them and tried to reassure them." She did not invite me to accompany her.

What a relief really. It's best for her, their seasoned caseworker, to deal single-handed with such a grave situation. But it's a bit surprising she doesn't seem remotely ashamed of herself or abashed. She's not in the least self-reproachful on account of her fatal miscalculation yesterday evening.

I didn't do much that morning, apart from writing up an account of what had occurred in the Kellies' casepaper and re-reading some of the latter so as to try to understand the situation better and decide whether anyone could possibly have foreseen what would occur. The atmosphere of crisis pervading the Agency prevented anyone in the building from doing much but discussing what had happened.

"I must say, I myself did just wonder," I ventured at one stage to Nell and Godfrey in the General Office, "whether really Gladys shouldn't have let her, advised her, to go to the Salvation Army hostel last night. It did occur to me something just might happen – so of course I got round there as fast as I could this morning."

154

Nell said nothing, but Godfrey responded encouragingly:

"How very astute of you Hilary. What a pity it wasn't you on duty yesterday instead of Glad."

He's not being sarcastic.

Later I was further encouraged by Ann remarking:

"You certainly were quick off the mark this morning, Hilary. You must have had some premonition that something awful was going to happen."

"Yes, well I suppose I sort of did," I replied humbly; and Ann added:

"That sort of intuition can be a very valuable attribute in a caseworker." She proceeded to give a lengthy, detailed illustration of this point from her own casework experience. I didn't listen.

Chapter 35

After dinner everyone seemed to disappear. Gladys was still out dealing with the Kelly children, Godfrey went to visit a Client and Monica summoned the others to her office for a Casework Tools and Techniques Discussion.

"It's one of the things we do regularly once a fortnight," Ann explained. "Those of us who aren't Probationers, that is."

Is there no end to the discussions? Hardly a day's passed since I came without some sort of meeting being held.

I decided I had better do something practical so I cycled off to see the Carters – precisely why I was not sure. No one was at home – at least nobody answered the door – so I went down to the Waterfront which I had not yet seen. I returned to the Agency at tea-time feeling refreshed and carefree. When, therefore, shortly after tea Clara told me Monica wanted to see me I went down to her office quite happily. Presumably she wanted to tell me what had happened to the Kelly children and what, if anything, my future role with them would be.

Monica was seated behind her desk staring down at her clasped hands, stretched out before her, as though she wanted to avoid looking at me. The top of her desk was bare but for the scribbling-pad – perhaps to show she intended to give me her undivided attention. She invited me to sit down then, looking away from me again, began:

"This is not going to be very pleasant I'm afraid, Hilary." She spoke even more slowly and expressionlessly than usual. The shock of her words shattered my shell of tranquility. "In the light of what happened this morning," she went on, "we have felt obliged to talk over your work again and carefully weigh up your potentialities as a caseworker." She paused.

"Yes," I responded.

So they weren't discussing casework tools and techniques at all. Ann was lying. Godfrey's right – she is two-faced.

I stared at the cobweb pattern on the scribbling-pad.

One, two, three, four strands...So yet again I've been the object of their searing scrutiny, ruthless probing...Five, six, seven strands. Now they're lines of sound: a high-pitched, wavering violin melody in a minor key.

"And we all felt that the matters I have raised with you already are too grave to be disregarded – especially in view of what has just happened."

The Kellies? What's their disaster got to do with my potentialities as a caseworker? What happened to them wasn't my fault.

"It is the policy of this Agency," she continued somewhat more briskly, "as I explained to you yesterday, to make continuous assessments of the progress of new workers and at the end of the first week to attempt some initial evaluation. We consider the Probationer in the light of the testimonials received about him. For it is sometimes the case that what has been said about a person beforehand is not sufficiently borne out by the quality of his work on arrival." She looked pointedly at me.

The violin melody has swerved up an octave.

"In such cases we have to carefully consider whether we ought to tell the Probationer our doubts about his capacity for the work here," she said, then stopped.

"Yes I see," I murmured.

"As I explained, we do this as much for the Probationer's sake as ours," she resumed, "as it is unfair to leave a Probationer for any length of time under the misapprehension that his progress is satisfactory when in fact we doubt whether he can ever hope to become accepted as a qualified worker at this Agency." Again

156

she paused and scrutinized me, her expression non-committal.

*Does she enjoy making such pronouncements? She must
do as she's actually only repeating and adding to what
she's said before.*

"In your case, Hilary," she went on, her speech tempo slowing
down again, "I have already indicated why we have hesitations
about you – hesitations expressed by everyone at yesterday's
meeting. We are inclined to doubt whether you can ever really
hope to become a successful caseworker. There is, we feel, this
basic anxiety; these deep, unconscious conflicts, dating perhaps
from very early in your life. They impair your ability to help
other problem-ridden people as a caseworker should. You are
tense and perpetually in bondage to your own problems so you
are never free to regard other people's problems objectively. This
means that you find it very hard to make decisions and take real
initiative."

*But what about all the initiative I've shown over the
Kellies and over getting Charly Dale fixed up with clothes,
and impressing Willy Carter's probation officer? She's not
being fair.*

As though reading my mind, Monica went on, "Yesterday, I
gather, you did manage to perform some quite practical tasks
for poor Mrs Kelly. But I'm afraid this doesn't alter what I've said.
The trouble I'm afraid is that your underlying personal insecurity
led you to try to rid yourself of it, or rather to gloss it over, by
making someone else dependent on you, thus boosting your
self-assurance. And with what fatal results! No one, of course, is
blaming you – or anyone else – for this morning's tragic events.
However, had you been a little less tense and rather more
observant yesterday at the Kellies' – less over-anxious and self-
absorbed – you might have discerned – foreseen hence managed
to prevent – what subsequently occurred this morning. Do you
see what I mean?"

*No I don't. She's very unjust. However could I have
guessed what would happen even if I had been feeling
quite objective and relaxed? Anyway, if anyone's to
blame it's surely Gladys, though there's no point in
saying so – she'd only accuse me of being defensive and
insecure.*

I just nodded.

Those two thicker cobweb strands are the oboe and viola's entry point into the melody. Now the violin's modulated into a different key and started to play a discordant descant.

Monica continued:

"Not that I'm saying all this is a conscious process on your part; but that, as this morning reveals, does not make it any less dangerous. On the contrary, it makes it if anything worse. And that is the crux of the matter. You have so much to grapple with in your own unconscious life, Hilary, that I'm afraid, despite your intelligence and powers of observation, you're not as yet capable of being genuinely helpful to other problem-ridden people – don't you agree?"

By now I was too dejected to feel resentful or argumentative.

"Perhaps," I muttered. "It's hard to know for sure about one's own feelings."

"I do so agree," she replied, possibly relieved that I had not embarked on a lengthy, strenuous self-defence. "And I am glad you realise this. It makes my own task a little easier and less disagreeable. Mrs Kelly is – was – just one among many Clients. But you can see, can't you, how, because of your own inner conflicts, you endangered rather than helped her. The same sort of thing could happen again in different ways with other Clients." She broke off for an instant; then, gazing away past me out of the window, stated very slowly, "We do have such a serious duty towards other people. And we have a duty towards ourselves too. You, Hilary," (now she looked back at me, speaking faster) "have not, I feel, been here quite long enough for us to be able to say categorically that you must give up and leave immediately."

My dejection lightened a trifle.

The violin has slipped into harmony with the other instruments.

"Indeed," she went on, "we always try not to be categorical, but to help those whose talents we feel lie in other directions to see for themselves that they have not chosen the right work. You may remember that when we first talked together I told you it is essential for caseworkers to be happy in their work. You, Hilary, are not I think really happy here with us, are you?"

The tune's faded. The cobweb's back. The seventh strand merges with the sixth half-way round.

I mumbled. Monica appeared satisfied with this response and went on:

"Even so, I, and the rest of us, would hesitate to say for certain that you could never possibly hope to become an effective social caseworker. At this stage we can only offer you our carefully considered opinion and urge you to think over very seriously the recommendations we feel obliged to make – for your own good and for the good of all concerned. In short, we do not say you *must* leave – we try never to say this. We only ask you to weigh up very carefully what I have just said." she paused, then added, "This is such demanding, exacting work, for which only a few, when all is said and done, are really destined. We cannot say with absolute certainty that you have chosen the wrong career, and that no amount of training and effort on your part would ever enable you to succeed in it." She looked hard at me, then resumed, "You can leave us if you agree with the views I have just expressed. But if you are convinced we are mistaken and that this is the work you should do and can be happy doing we will reserve our judgement for the moment."

She stopped, then summed up:

"I have told you how we feel. You can leave us or stay. We refuse to tell you what to do. It is you, Hilary, who must choose."